American royalty

Lost in thought about what that might mean, Melanie didn't hear the red Jaguar convertible until it sped around the blind corner. Nearly crashing into her rental car, the dark-haired driver made a brilliant save at the last minute…before swerving in her direction!

Melanie gasped, but before she cold jump out of the way, he swerved again. She barely got a look at his hard-chiseled features, softened only by surprise, before the Jaguar zoomed away from her.

"What are you, some kind of lunatic?" she yelled after him, her heart pounding double time.

Coming to a screeching stop, the Jaguar rammed into reverse, taillights glaring red. This time she did jump…sideways…landing precariously at the edge of the drop-off….

PATRICIA ROSEMOOR

SLATER HOUSE

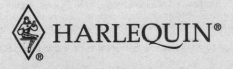

TORONTO • NEW YORK • LONDON
AMSTERDAM • PARIS • SYDNEY • HAMBURG
STOCKHOLM • ATHENS • TOKYO • MILAN • MADRID
PRAGUE • WARSAW • BUDAPEST • AUCKLAND

ISBN 0-373-22924-0

SLATER HOUSE

www.eHarlequin.com

Printed in U.S.A.

ABOUT THE AUTHOR

Patricia Rosemoor has always had a fascination with dangerous love. In addition to her more than forty Harlequin Intrigue novels, she also writes for Harlequin Blaze and Silhouette Bombshell, bringing a different mix of thrills and chills and romance to each line.

She's won a Golden Heart from Romance Writers of America and Reviewers' Choice and Career Achievement Awards from *Romantic Times BOOKclub*, and she teaches writing popular fiction and suspense-thriller writing in the fiction writing department of Columbia College Chicago. Check out her Web site: www.PatriciaRosemoor.com. You can contact Patricia either via e-mail at Patricia@PatriciaRosemoor.com, or through the publisher at Patricia Rosemoor, c/o Harlequin/Silhouette Books, 233 Broadway, New York, NY 10279.

Books by Patricia Rosemoor

CAST OF CHARACTERS

Melanie Pierce—The documentary filmmaker realizes her whole life is a lie when she learns of a grandfather and other family members who were supposedly dead.

Ross Bennet—The restoration architect wants back into Slater House for personal reasons.

John Grey—The private investigator delivers the news to Melanie and then ends up dead.

Olivia Pierce—She sets off to rescue her daughter, only to run into the killer.

Frederick Slater—Melanie's grandfather is the same controlling man who drove her mother away from Slater House—but did he do more than try to control her?

Martin Slater—Will Melanie's uncle do whatever it takes to get control of the Slater fortune?

Vincent Slater—Is Martin's son the one who will do anything to get rid of his competition?

Andrew Lennox—The head of the Slater legal team knows the family secrets—but is he using them to his own advantage?

Roger Johnson—Did the butler imagine himself as more than a servant in the Slater household?

Prologue

Fog-limned mountain peaks backed the abandoned wing of the gray stone mansion, making it look like something out of a horror movie.

A smile curled his lips at the comparison. It would be horrific for *her*.

Keeping to the shelter of shadows, he slipped inside. The full moon cast a silver-blue glow through the double-story windows, leaving a checkerboard of light. Easier to see her, to make certain all would happen as planned.

She would come, he thought, climbing the stairs. He'd made sure of it. She couldn't resist the temptation.

Always poking and prodding, sticking her patrician nose where it didn't belong...

Not for much longer.

Stopping at a window that gave him a view of the courtyard and gardens, he checked the time. Midnight. The witching hour. And there she was.

A pale robe covered her matching nightgown. Both glowed silver-blue as they floated on the wind, rising with the ebb and flow of air as if they would allow her to fly like an angel….

He nearly laughed out loud at the irony.

The moment she disappeared to enter the wing, he took a quick look around to make sure there were no prying eyes. Then he silently got into position. Everything was ready. His heart pumped faster as he heard her footsteps—light *tap-taps* across the debris-laden floor below—knowing this night he would be one step closer to his goal.

She stopped exactly where she was supposed to. Bent over to open the old trunk.

His mouth went dry and his heart threatened to burst from his chest as he manipulated the line he'd rigged. As the old chandelier broke free from the ceiling, the crystals tinkled in warning. Her head flew up, her pretty mouth opened, her eyes widened. She tried to get up and away, but she couldn't move fast enough. The chandelier crashed down on top of her, crystal knives biting into her flesh as the monstrosity pinned her to the floor.

Quickly, even as he heard a shouted "What was that?" from somewhere on the grounds, he pulled in the rigging and hid it in an old hassock that sat innocently near a window.

He took one last look at his handiwork. If only he could see her expression…but, alas, he had to save himself, to get away before he was caught.

Slipping through one of the hidden doors, he thought about who would be next.

Chapter One

"How did he hurt you?" Melanie Pierce asked.

An award-winning documentary video director, Melanie stood next to the camera, forgetting its presence and that of her camera operator and the small group of onlookers at the mouth of the alley. She focused on a young woman who'd been raped at knifepoint on the very spot where she now stood. Melanie cared about this story. She cared about them all. Perhaps that was why she had a talent for drawing out the truth from the most reluctant of subjects.

"…pinned me down with a knee in my back… then he did it…"

Melanie was producing *The Weaker Sex,* a documentary about women who'd gone beyond victimization and had made something positive of their lives. *The Weaker Sex* referred not to the women, but to the men who needed to use brute force to feel good about themselves.

"And then he left me there, bleeding…. I—I heard him laugh as he walked away…."

A moment of silence and the victim's expression hardened to that of a survivor, and Melanie knew the interview was over.

"Thank you for being so candid," Melanie said softly, stopping the recording. "You're very brave for being part of this project."

Anger flashed through the young woman's expression. "I would've killed the bastard if I could've."

Melanie nodded but didn't comment.

It was only after her subject left and the equipment was packed up that Melanie realized that while the crowd had dispersed, an older man remained. Judging from his tailored suit, he wasn't from this neighborhood in Chicago. He was coming straight at her as if he had a mission.

"Can I help you?"

"You're Melanie Pierce," he said in a gravelly voice, his rheumy gaze traveling to her red hair, which she'd pulled back from her face and had dramatized with a few streaks of magenta and magenta-lacquered chopsticks.

A fan of her work or a naysayer? she wondered suspiciously. She too often had to deal with people who took issue with her documentaries, so she was understandably wary when someone approached her uninvited.

"I know who I am," she said evenly. "What about you?"

"John Grey, private investigator."

That jolted her spine straight. "You're investigating what? Me? Why?"

"Let's get a cuppa coffee and talk."

Melanie laughed. "You're kidding, right? I'm a big-city girl, Mr. Grey. What makes you think I would go anywhere with a stranger?"

"I had coffee with your mother, Olivia, yesterday."

The mention of her mother quickly sobered her. "What does Mom have to do with this?" Suddenly the man appeared to be a threat. "Who hired you?"

Grey eyed her camera operator. "It's…um…private."

The back of her neck prickled.

Waving away her colleague, who hauled off the equipment to his car, Melanie faced the P.I. "Say what you have to say."

He shrugged. "So be it. I was hired to find you—"

"I got that part."

"By your grandfather, Frederick Slater. Your mother's father."

"My mother's father died when she was a teenager. And his name was Matt Pierce." She took a deep breath in an effort to calm herself. "I'm afraid you've got the wrong girl."

"I'm afraid not. When she was only eighteen, Olivia Slater ran away from home."

The back of her neck prickled some more.

He went on. "Olivia got a job in Chicago and went to school at night. She became quite successful in real estate and bought a big home for the two of you."

"That part is right, but—"

"It's *all* right. Your mother's been lying to you

your whole life. I knew her in her old one. Trust me, Olivia Slater and Olivia Pierce are the same woman. You got a family, Ms. Pierce. Not only do you have a maternal grandfather, but there's your uncle Martin and his wife, Eleanor, and their son, Vincent, and your late uncle Nicholas's wife, Helen. They all live at Slater House."

Her stomach clenched but Melanie shook her head in denial. "Mom wouldn't lie to me. If what you're saying is true, you would be at *her* to go back, not me."

"Your mother don't want to be found—"

"What bull!"

"One way to find out. Come to North Carolina and give your grandfather a chance to welcome you into the family."

A family she hadn't known she had.

If it was true.

"Look, I don't know what your game is…" Melanie backed away toward the street and knocked into one of the black resin garbage cans, whose lid chattered in protest before slamming shut again. "But go look for another playmate."

"Your grandfather is quite ill. He was hoping that while he still could…" Grey cleared his throat and changed tactics. "Frederick Slater is as close to American royalty as it gets. Your mother walked out on the Slater fortune. You don't gotta."

"Lies." Heart thumping, Melanie continued putting distance between them. "All lies."

"I'm staying at the Drake until tomorrow. Call me."

Without answering, she rushed away and got into her car. It couldn't be true. None of it.

Even as she denied the man's story, Melanie remembered the weird vibes that had come off her mother the day before, as if something had been eating at her. And when she'd questioned Mom about it, her mother had laughed and somehow closed off those disturbing emotions.

Could Grey be telling the truth?

Melanie gripped the steering wheel so hard her knuckles whitened. Mom had always taught her that honesty was the best policy. If Grey's claims were true, it seemed that policy applied to everyone but her mother.

Needing reassurance, Melanie wasted no time in driving to the Ravenswood neighborhood where she'd grown up. The pale mauve frame house with the big white porch wrapping around two sides was still home even though she had her own apartment. She used her key to get in and called out, "Mom?"

"In here, Mel."

Entering the living room, classically decorated in mauve and cream, Melanie saw her mother put down her magazine and felt, as always, as if she were looking into a mirror. Her mother's face was heart-shaped, her round eyes a vivid blue, her lips full enough to be fashionable…and curved in a wide smile as if nothing were wrong.

Her pulse spiked as she said, "A funny thing happened on my way here, Mom."

"Funny weird or funny ha-ha?"

"Not sure. You tell me." She stopped several feet in front of her mother. "Does the name Slater make you laugh?"

Her mother's horrified expression said it all.

The prickling practically made the small hairs at the back of her neck dance.

"Mom, is it true? Is your father alive? And did you have brothers you never told me about?"

"That bastard! I should have known better. He always was a weasel. He wasn't supposed to find you. He was supposed to drop the investigation right here! He was supposed to tell my father I died in a car accident winter before last!"

Melanie's world suddenly spun off its axis and her knees turned to jelly. She gripped the back of a club chair so she wouldn't fall. It was true then, everything Grey had told her. The one person in the world she thought she could trust *had* been lying to her all her life.

"I—I don't understand." Her mother wanted people to believe she was dead…just as she'd made Melanie believe *they* were dead. Why? "Talk to me, Mom. Tell me what's going on."

"I—I can't."

The catch in her mother's voice tightened Melanie's throat.

A sense of dread whispered through her. Her mother's dread. She could feel the fear as if it were her own. It had always been this way, ever since she could remember. She could read her mother…sense her emotions…but it was only a one-way street. Her mother couldn't read Melanie in return.

"Whatever happened," Melanie choked out, "that was more than twenty-five years ago."

"Twenty-five years is nothing. I buried the past. Let it *stay* buried. Mel, you have to promise me you'll keep away from those people and that place."

Those people? That place? Her mom's family. Her mom's childhood home. What was so horrible that she didn't even want to talk about it?

Her mother rose from her chair and moved toward Melanie. "Sweetheart, you have everything you need here. Please leave well enough alone."

Her pulse jagged and Melanie felt the back of her throat grow thick. Waves of something dark and terrible coming from her mother enveloped her, threatening to smother her.

Danger?

Was her mother in danger?

Despite the wavering smile that trembled on her mother's lips, she certainly was terrified. Never having felt anything like this from her mother before, Melanie was, too.

"Hey, Mom, don't worry about it." She tried to put on a good face so her mother would calm down. "You're right. The past can stay buried. I have everything I need right here."

The darkness eased a bit.

"Then you won't call John Grey?"

"I won't call him."

And eased some more.

"Good. Good."

But it wasn't good, whatever it was that had driven

her mother from her home and family. And now John Grey had caught up to her mother, and she had paid him off to say she was dead.

Dead!

Why?

Wanting to put her mother's mind at peace, Melanie said, "Hey, my new documentary is taking up all my time, anyway. I probably won't be home much for the next few days. If you need me, call me on my cell, okay?"

"Sure…" Her mother reached out and smoothed a stray lock of hair from Melanie's face. Her fingers trembled. "Mel, you won't call Grey, right? You promise?"

"I said I wouldn't." Swallowing hard so that she wouldn't cry, Melanie hugged her mother, murmuring, "Love you, Mom."

The dark thing was safely caged inside her mother again. Somehow she'd seemed to compartmentalize her emotions…something she'd probably been doing for twenty-five years. Melanie could no longer read her.

"I love you, Mel."

Her mother sounded relieved but Melanie felt anything but as she left the house and drove to her Logan Square neighborhood. She tried to keep her rising anxiety in check, to segue to thinking about her documentary, but she simply couldn't.

While she and her mother had been enough for each other all these years, Melanie had always wondered what it might be like to have a larger family. And now she found out she had one and her mother was afraid of her getting to know them. *Why...why... why?* What had happened to make her mother run? To keep her afraid after all these years?

Melanie simply couldn't fathom a good enough reason as she entered her century-old apartment decorated in secondhand chic. She headed straight for her office with its wall of framed movie posters.

Sliding down into the old leather-and-wood manager's chair behind her mahogany desk, Melanie switched her gaze to the framed photos that sat on its surface—of both her and her mother. One had been taken on her first day of school. The other when she'd graduated from college. They might have different styles—her mother's was classic, while hers was right now—but they looked so much alike with their fiery red hair, blue eyes and porcelain skin that they could almost be the same person. She didn't think she could know anyone better....

Or so she had thought until today.

She couldn't help herself. Instead of watching footage as she'd meant to do, she got on the Internet. It wouldn't hurt to Google her own family history.

Thirty minutes later she sat back and thought about what she'd learned. That Slater House had been completed by running a railroad spur line to the center of Slater Woods, a half hour out of Asheville. That industrialist Zachary Slater—her great-great-grandfather—had invited all his wealthy friends and rivals to a Fourth of July celebration to see the ninety-nine-room marvel and to tour the adjacent farm and vineyards. That, while all of the farm and much of Slater

Woods had been sold off and developed, Slater House and the vineyard had remained in the hands of the Slater family for one hundred and twenty-five years.

American royalty.

This was the legacy from which her mother had run.

And then there was Frederick Slater himself, said to be one of the wealthiest men in the country. By all accounts, her grandfather wasn't an easy man. He was demanding and controlling, traits indicative of his financial success. And indicative of his failure with his family, at least with her free-spirited mother, Melanie thought. She herself would hate anyone trying to control her.

She might think her grandfather had controlled his daughter right out of his house and his life if she hadn't sensed the darkness in her mother.

Melanie tried to distance herself so she could look at the details impartially as if she were shooting one of her documentaries.

Olivia Pierce was a strong woman with definite opinions. She would stand up to anyone and often had, especially if it was in her daughter's defense, Melanie thought. Her mother was devoted to her, had done everything for her. It had always just been the two of them since her father had died before she was born. Melanie had always been okay with that....

Until now, when she learned that not only had her mother had been living a lie, but she had, as well.

"YOU BASTARD! You took twenty thousand dollars from me and then betrayed me!" Olivia Pierce stormed past John Grey into his hotel suite and threw her Gucci bag on a table.

He'd come up in the world, enough to afford a luxury hotel on the Magnificent Mile. But no matter that he wore tailored suits and surrounded himself with fancy appointments, he was slime.

"How dare you impugn my integrity," he responded, amusement laced through the drawled words.

"You approached my daughter."

"You didn't make her part of our deal."

It took everything in her power not to slap him. "I told you the investigation stopped dead with me." She hadn't known if he'd found out about Melanie or not, and she certainly hadn't wanted to alert him.

"And so it did stop with you," he said. "The report of your death reached your father this morning. He was suitably grief-stricken. As to your daughter—he knows about her existence, but not that I'd actually found her. I merely followed up on a lead already in my possession by making the meet."

"You always were a weasel, looking out for yourself and no one else. If it hadn't been for you, Father would never have known about…" Olivia let her words trail off in a sob. Bringing up the past wouldn't solve her present situation. "Did you tell him about Mel? Has she called you?" Dear Lord, she hoped not.

"Not yet…but I told her I'd be here till tomorrow morning."

"She's not going to call you." Olivia tried to believe that, but a niggle of doubt worried at her. "But if she does…find a way to shut down her interest."

"That's not what I'm being paid for."

"I'll pay you. You owe me this, John." Olivia dug into her bag, pulled out an envelope fat with cash and handed it to him. "Will this do it for you? Will this help you talk her out of going and keep knowledge of her whereabouts from my father? You could tell him she disappeared without a trace just like I did twenty-five years ago."

Olivia would pay anything, do anything, to keep her daughter safe. Luckily, the private investigator didn't demand more than she'd brought with her.

Slipping the envelope into a drawer, Grey said, "You realize, even if your daughter doesn't call me, she knows about your family and where to find them."

Olivia prayed she could somehow make the break permanent. She simply needed some time to figure out how to handle Mel.

"Just buy me some time, John. Please."

Grey's expression softened and Olivia remembered he'd once been fond of her. She'd been a kid then, wild and reckless, earning disapproval from her siblings and father. She guessed that was what he'd liked about her. Though he made a living off Frederick Slater, Olivia knew Grey didn't like her father, so maybe…

"If it comes to that," he said, "I'll do what I can."

The best she could hope for, Olivia decided, taking her leave.

Blind to the window displays of the exclusive shops as she walked along North Michigan Avenue, she tried to keep Slater House and her father and all that had happened twenty-five years ago at bay. She'd locked up those memories and had shoved them back to a distant part of her mind, almost as if she'd erased them. But John Grey had opened the door…and she only hoped Melanie didn't find her way in.

Olivia told herself to concentrate, to stay in control. She wasn't eighteen and powerless anymore. She had a comfortable life and a daughter who would make any mother proud. After all these years, she couldn't go back.

And neither could Melanie.

Chapter Two

Melanie's sleep was restless, her dreams elusive, but all had to do with the imposing house that was her heritage and the imposing man who was her grandfather.

Dreams turned to nightmares and her mother ran through them screaming....

By dawn, Melanie was exhausted but knew what she had to do. No matter what her mother wanted, she had to face both house and grandfather.

Remembering how the waves of her mother's dark emotions had enveloped her, Melanie could come to only one conclusion. The past had the possibility of putting her mother in some kind of danger in the present...and Melanie had to see to her mother's safe future. She couldn't chance anything happening to the one person who was her everything.

She'd promised not to call John Grey, so she didn't. *Better that way,* she thought. *No warnings.*

Her job made her good at reading people. And at drawing them out. She wanted gut reactions when she appeared. She would approach this like a new project and look at these Slater relatives—these strangers—with distance.

Finding her new digital camcorder, she packed it in her shoulder bag along with some other recording equipment that might come in handy.

Then she packed a bigger bag with a few changes of clothing and simply left, flying to Asheville on her own. Two commuter-size planes later, she walked out onto the tarmac and hurried inside the terminal to luggage retrieval and the rental car station. Having gotten driving directions from an Internet site, she immediately headed for the estate.

The air was cool and a breeze played through the trees as she drove into a more rural hilly area. Coming from an overcrowded city like Chicago, she was amazed at all the land that seemed to have nothing but trees and wildlife on it. Passing through a small town called Slater Corners—lots of little shops and restaurants and some other businesses—she sailed by the sign that marked her entrance to Slater Woods.

Breathing here seemed to take a bit more work, and she reminded herself that she was in the mountains, a fact that became more obvious as she drove along a road that took her deeper into the woods and up a series of hills. A bridge crossed a stream that cut through the property and when she looked to her right, the view made her exclaim softly. A lovely narrow waterfall trickled down a hillside to pool in the ribbon of water below.

But as she rounded a sharp curve, the vista before her opened between trees to reveal landscaped grounds and several garden areas that softened the three-story gray stone house and attached stables. She slammed on the brakes, slid out from behind the driver's seat and walked forward, closer to a drop-off, so she could better see the estate. Even though she had done her research, she wasn't prepared for the sheer enormity of the ninety-nine-room dwelling that looked more like a European palace than a place where people actually lived.

American royalty.

And she wasn't prepared for the sense of familiarity…almost as if she remembered Slater House…

Lost in thought about what that might mean, she didn't hear the red Jaguar convertible until it sped around the blind corner. Nearly crashing into her rental car, the dark-haired driver made a brilliant save at the last minute…before swerving in her direction!

Melanie gasped, but before she could jump out of the way, he swerved again. She barely got a look at his hard-chiseled features softened only slightly by surprise, before the Jaguar zoomed away from her.

"What are you, some kind of lunatic?" she yelled after him, her heart pounding double time. "This isn't a speedway, so slow down before you kill someone!"

Coming to a screeching stop, the Jaguar rammed into Reverse, taillights glaring red. This time she did jump…sideways…landing precariously at the edge of the drop-off.

Arms flailing, heart in her throat, Melanie tried to

regain her balance as she heard a car door open and shoes scuffle. Her foot skidded in the soft earth and she felt herself starting to slide downward. In desperation, she lunged for a nearby tree trunk, but rather than rough bark, her hand met air as the earth moved under her feet.

Suddenly a hand, a manacle of steel, surrounded her wrist and jerked her to a bone-jarring stop.

"Slow down before you kill yourself." Standing on firm footing, the Jaguar driver threw her command back at her.

"Me? You're the one who—"

"I could let go," he warned her.

Was he kidding? Or was that a threat?

He appeared serious enough. His mouth was turned down, his expression grim.

Melanie drew on her reserves and used his grip as leverage to pull herself back up to his level until they were sunglasses to sunglasses.

"First…" She gasped. "Thanks. Second…were you trying to kill me or what?"

"If that had been my intention, you'd be dead."

The way he said it so matter-of-factly put a lump in her throat. Who the hell was he? Someone demented, certainly.

"First," he went on, "you never stop on a blind curve because that could get you killed, not to mention the driver who has a heart attack when your car being where it doesn't belong surprises the hell out of him."

"If you hadn't been going so fast—"

"My turn! Second. You don't blame someone else for your own thoughtlessness."

Melanie was doubly angry because she knew he was right. "Who are you, anyway?"

"I could ask the same of you," he countered. "Are you Vincent's newest woman?"

Vincent. She remembered the private investigator saying she had a cousin by that name.

Wanting a better look at him, she nested her sunglasses in the front of her hair and wished he would do the same. He didn't, though, merely continued to glare at her—at least she assumed he was glaring since she couldn't actually see his eyes. She wondered if he was one of her relatives. Surely he wasn't one of the servants, not driving a Jaguar XK8.

When she responded, "I'm my own woman," his eyebrows raised above the dark glasses.

"Promising," he murmured, his low voice raising the flesh on her arms.

His gaze narrowed on her face and she could swear she saw a reaction before he hid it.

Half expecting him to hit on her, Melanie was surprised when he backed off toward the open car door and slid in behind the wheel.

"Better move that car before someone does smack into you," he growled, then roared off just as fast as he had before.

He…whoever he might be.

Before she became target practice for any more vehicles coming around the corner, she got back in her car, muttering, "Welcome to the Slater estate, Melanie."

ROSS BENNET glanced into his rearview mirror and saw the other car move off from the curve. Damn, the woman had surprised him. Her looks had, too.

Something about her had seemed familiar, and when he'd gotten a good look at her without the sunglasses, he'd seen the resemblance to Olivia. It had been twenty-five years…but how could he forget? This young woman had to be Olivia's daughter, Melanie, whom he'd heard about recently.

He drove straight toward the south wing, which had been abandoned half a century ago, no doubt because a house this size took a fortune to run and the family simply wasn't big enough to fill the rooms they already had. Everyone had been surprised when the old man had decided he'd wanted to restore rather than tear down the wing with its myriad structural problems.

That was what losing a grandchild would do to a man like Frederick Slater. He needed to eradicate the condition that had caused the tragedy. Ross had snagged the job a few days ago, a mere month after Louisa's death. No one knew why the girl had gone to the abandoned wing that fateful night….

Her death had left only one grandchild, Vincent, as the heir to the Slater legacy.

Until now.

John Grey must have found Melanie Pierce, after all. Not that the P.I. had said so when he'd informed the old man Olivia was dead. Gossip was rife on the estate and Ross was still privy to what went on there. After the news of Olivia's death, the house had been more like a tomb than usual. Ross figured Melanie would stir things up with her magenta-streaked hair, multiple ear piercings and Bohemian clothing.

Ross would love to be a fly on the wall when Frederick got a load of the tattoo on her hip peeking out from her low-rider pants.

Parking near the abandoned wing, he approached on foot. He hadn't counted on the triumph of winning the project bid being tarnished by memories. Then again, the past was the real reason he'd been determined to get this job. Once upon a time his grandfather had been in charge of the grounds, his father in charge of the stables, but that had been twenty-five years ago.

For years he'd wanted a way to have free access to the estate again, and finally he did.

He figured the only reason Frederick Slater had hired him for the restoration job was that long ago Ross had saved the old man's favorite dog, who'd run into a possum. Ten years old at the time, Ross had chased away the wild animal and had carried the wounded dog nearly a mile back to the house. The old man had given him twenty dollars and a promise to repay him in a more significant way someday.

Whatever else you could say about Frederick Slater, he didn't forget his promises, and Ross hadn't hesitated to take any advantage he could.

Though he, like his father and grandfather before him, was now working for the old man, Ross saw it as a business deal, far different than working for him as one of the servant class. He might not have Slater's money, but in his mind he was now the old man's equal. The renovation had to be perfect. No missteps. No more accidents.

This was the type of opportunity that only came around once in a lifetime. The kind of job that could make a restoration architect's reputation.

And more important than that, it could finally lead him to the truth of what had really happened the night before his family had been thrown off the estate.

AS IF SHE WERE SHOOTING footage of Slater House, Melanie panned its length to absorb every detail from the limestone facade to the peaked roof above to the formal gardens below.

Movement caught her eye and she realized someone on the second floor was peering out at her. She fought the urge to wave. And she forced herself to take the steps forward necessary to reach the front doors. Of carved mahogany, they were perhaps twelve or more feet in height. The brass knocker was elaborate, a gargoyle of a face that bade her no welcome.

Would she really receive any welcome here?

One way to find out. She clanked brass against brass and a moment later the door creaked open to reveal a middle-aged man with silver wings at his temples and a jowly face that reminded her of a bulldog.

He gaped and his brown eyes grew round. "Miss Olivia? But you're…you're…"

"Melanie." The man had obviously known Mom.

"Ah, you're the daughter," he murmured, stepping back. "We weren't expecting you. My, my, don't you look just like her. Come in, miss. Mr. Frederick will be thrilled to see you."

Mr. Frederick.... Not a relative, then. She eyed the man's black vest, long-sleeved white shirt and tie that undoubtedly served as a uniform.

"And you are—"

"Johnson. Mr. Frederick's butler." He looked out to where her car was parked. "Your bags? If you give me your keys, miss, I shall fetch them right after I bring you to the family."

Family....

Her stomach lurched as she handed over the car keys.

Stay impartial, she reminded herself. *Look at everything with a director's eye. Think of this experience as research for a new video project, not as a welcome home.*

Melanie followed the butler across a foyer that was larger than her entire apartment. The floor was marble; the ceiling was arched and perhaps fifteen feet high. They crossed through a conservatory with a burbling fountain flanked by twin seating areas and myriad tropical plants. Light filtered down from above—the ceiling like that in a greenhouse—in such a way that she could shoot footage in here without artificial lighting.

Her footsteps slowed as voices drifted out to her from an adjoining room. Not happy voices, but the sounds of disagreement. Johnson didn't seem a bit deterred as he swept right into a parlor filled with antiques, artwork, a baby grand piano and several people. Not that any of them seemed to notice her as, her heart pounding, she stopped dead at the threshold.

The butler loudly cleared his throat. "Ahem!"

"What is it, Johnson?" came a querulous voice.

"You have a guest, Mr. Frederick."

Melanie inspected her grandfather. Though the silver-haired man was on the thin side, an undeniable strength emanated from him. Blue eyes that were still sharp quickly found her. Eyes that would capture the lens and the audience on the other side of the camera.

"Who is that you have there? Olivia?" he queried with a gasp.

Before the butler could answer, she stepped forward. "I'm Melanie Pierce."

"Melanie?" His voice quavered just a bit and he seemed confused. Then his eyes took on a sudden sheen of emotion. "You're Olivia's Melanie?"

Melanie's nerves felt on fire as a hush fell over the room and all eyes zeroed in on her.

"Olivia is my mother," she agreed, stopping just far enough away that she could see them all at the same time. No sign of the deranged Jaguar driver.

A small relief.

"Welcome, my dear, welcome."

Her grandfather made as if he wanted to hug her, but Melanie stepped back and offered him her hand instead. He frowned but covered fast and took the hand possessively in both of his.

"Is that really Olivia's daughter?" one of the two women in the room asked.

While pretty, she did nothing to play up her looks.

Her brown hair was pulled back in a twist and her dress was of an unremarkable flower print.

"Just look at her," the other said, not bothering to hide her snide tone. "If her hair and clothing weren't so outrageous, she would be a dead ringer for her mother."

"That's enough, Eleanor! Melanie is my grand-daughter, a real Slater!"

At that pronouncement the energy in the room startled Melanie. Was it merely instinct or more? she wondered, staring at Eleanor, a striking blonde with a taste for designer clothing and jewelry. Melanie was used to picking up intense vibes from her mother, but not around other people, not like this. Nerves. No doubt that was all she was feeling.

"*Eleanor* is a real Slater, Father," said the man with the receding hairline who must be her uncle Martin. He fit his wife in style, dressing like a wealthy executive. "She has been since the day she became my bride."

Her grandfather ignored him and gazed into Melanie's face. "I'm so glad you accepted my invitation to come to Slater House. Unfortunately, John Grey didn't inform me."

"Because I chose to come without informing him."

Frederick Slater digested the explanation before nodding his approval. "Ah, you wanted to catch us off guard." He grinned. "Good girl! Definitely a real Slater."

Melanie wasn't so sure she liked being called any kind of a Slater. "My name is Pierce," she reminded him.

"No matter what you call yourself, my dear—my blood runs through your veins."

Actually, his claim ran a chill through Melanie's veins. She'd been uneasy since entering the room. As much as she tried to tell herself it was simply nerves kicking up, she didn't actually feel nervous now that she was in the middle of things. So what was the scoop here?

"You'll have to be patient with us while the staff gets on board with your arrival," Frederick said. "We haven't had time to prepare properly for you."

"No need to fuss," Melanie said, feeling resentment—and something stronger?—pound at her from the others. She was glad to see Johnson stop in the doorway, her suitcase and shoulder bag in hand. Relief swept through her. "I have everything I need with me."

Her grandfather chuckled. "If that's all you brought, I seriously doubt it. No matter. I have someone who can deal with any difficulty."

Was he saying she was difficult? She'd just arrived unexpectedly and already he had plans for her?

"I can only stay for a few days," she informed him. "My work awaits."

"Which can't be as important as newfound family."

"Family doesn't pay the rent," she said, keeping her tone light.

"Well…but it can, my dear. That all depends on you."

The moment money was mentioned, Melanie felt the very air grow thick with unwelcome vibes. The others were staring at her as if trying to get inside her head. As if they wanted to know her intentions when it came to the family finances.

Was that why they thought she was here? Out of greed? They couldn't be more wrong, of course. She was happy making her own way, something she'd learned to do from her mother. But let them think what they would so that her real motives would go undetected.

"We'll see how things go," she said coyly, turning her smile from her grandfather to her uncle and aunts, who looked self-satisfied at her answer.

Good.

"Shall I escort Miss Melanie to her room?" Johnson asked. "If the Rose Suite would be suitable…?"

"It'll do," her grandfather said. "For now. Get yourself comfortable, my dear. Unfortunately, I have some business to attend to this afternoon. Can't be avoided. But we'll get to know you better tonight. You can use the time to rest or to explore the house and grounds. Johnson will see to your needs. Cocktails at six. Be punctual!"

"Six it is." She crossed to the butler.

"And, Melanie…"

"Yes?"

"Wear something more appropriate."

Clenching her jaw so she wouldn't disagree, Melanie waited until they were halfway up the stairs before muttering, "No doubt he means something not so Bohemian." The dressy casual style appealed to both her artistic and feminine sides.

"Mr. Frederick is a formal man."

Too bad she hadn't brought anything he would consider suitable. Oh, well, either he would relent or she would be eating in the kitchen with the servants, she supposed. Not that she would mind—she could probably learn a lot from them.

"These people," she said, eyeing the framed photographs on the wall as they ascended the stairs. "Are they all family?"

"Mostly."

"Oh, here's Mom!"

Melanie stopped to take a good look. Her mother wore a sea blue long dress and her red hair swung in a silky curve to her shoulders.

"That was taken at her high school graduation party, about a month before she disappeared for good. She was certainly stunning that night."

"And this one—my grandmother?" The woman looked like Mom did now.

"Indeed. Poor Miss Mildred. She contracted a virus that destroyed her heart when your mother was only fifteen. She was on a transplant list, and all the money in the world couldn't scare up another heart from someone with her rare blood type. Mr. Frederick was inconsolable after her death. No doubt the reason he so favored Miss Olivia was that she reminded him of his late wife."

When they arrived at the landing, Melanie asked, "Was the Rose Suite my mother's by any chance?"

"Actually, Miss Olivia occupied the Buttercup Suite, which overlooks the stables," the butler said, pointing down the hall in the opposite direction. "The one at the end of that corridor. No one has stayed in it since she left. No one has been allowed to change a thing. One of the maids cleans it weekly, though, and sets out fresh flowers. Poor Mr. Frederick. I'm certain he hoped that one day she would simply return and take up where she'd left off. And now he'll never have that chance."

Not wanting to give Johnson the chance to bring up her mother's car accident, Melanie asked, "What was Mom like as a child?"

The butler smiled. "For one, Miss Olivia was horse crazy and used to watch the equines being exercised as she studied in her window seat."

"You must have known her quite well."

"Miss Olivia made herself known to everyone without the usual family-servant restraints. Quite a free spirit she was," he added.

Free spirit? He wasn't describing *her* cautious mother.

"Here we are."

As he opened the door to her temporary quarters, Melanie couldn't help but be impressed by the size and beauty of the sitting room decorated in rose and cream. A pale love seat and rose-print club chair with footstool sat in front of a fireplace with a rose marble mantel.

"Your bedroom and bath are this way, miss." Johnson led the way and set down her bags next to a carved and painted wood wardrobe.

The bed, canopied and curtained in rose print, faced a semicircle of windows with a mountain view. Melanie glanced down at the grounds below. Still no sign of the red Jaguar or its driver. She poked her head in the bathroom and noted the claw-footed tub and pedestal sink with faucets that appeared to be made of gold.

The suite was like something out of a fairy tale. Not to her personal taste, perhaps—more to her mother's, if truth be told. Though she would prefer bold colors and a more contemporary feel, the suite was quite impressive.

"Is there anything I can get you, miss?"

"If I think of anything, I'll let you know. I may do what my grandfather suggested and just explore the grounds until it's time to get ready for dinner."

"Very good. If you need anything, pick up any telephone in the house, hit the intercom button and dial nine."

"I'll remember."

Melanie walked the butler to the door, and as he left, glanced back down the corridor, thinking she couldn't wait to search her mother's rooms, where hopefully, she would find a clue to the past.

Chapter Three

Getting into her mother's old quarters wasn't as easily accomplished as Melanie had hoped. By the time she freshened up, emptied her suitcases and got herself back in the hallway, two young maids had taken over the wing. Their cart was parked a few yards from the Buttercup Suite door. One of the maids dispensed fresh linens to a nearby room, while the other dusted a hall table.

Frustrated, Melanie decided her investigation would have to wait a while. In the meantime, she would look around the grounds and orient herself.

Remembering seeing outside doors in the salon where she'd met her relatives earlier, she approached the room with caution. It was now thankfully empty—no one to interrogate her—so she quickly walked through and let herself onto a long terrace that had a set of steps at each end.

Several other rooms held exits to the walkway—what kind of rooms Melanie could only speculate as she stood shock-still, coming to terms with the true immensity of the house. A wing spread from both sides of the larger main building, giving it a U shape. Gardens, a swimming pool and a smaller water feature—a fountain pouring water into a reflection pool—were set within the arms of the sprawling building.

One of the wings—the one farthest from the stables and therefore farthest from outside activity—looked to be in disrepair. Deserted, actually.

Unable to resist the temptation of checking it out—wondering what tales its forsaken walls told—Melanie hurried down the steps and crossed the path to the wing in question.

Halfway there, feeling as if someone were watching her, she hesitated and looked around. The only person she spotted moving across the grounds was a worker carrying a heavy bag of manure over his shoulder. He wasn't even looking her way.

Great. This was a great place to spur her already active imagination, Melanie thought, hurrying to the nearest doorway that would get her inside.

It was locked.

She tried the next one.

Locked.

And a third.

All locked.

Frustrated, really wanting to see the interior of the mysterious wing, she was circling around and looking for a way in when she came face-to-face with the red Jaguar parked on the other side.

So this was where its driver had been headed. Hmm. Interesting…and the nearby door stood open.

She entered a double-storied room, her gaze sweeping down its dusty length to the curved staircase and balcony on the opposite side. A weird feeling swept over her—a sense of familiarity—but before she could pursue that thought, a voice came out of the dark.

"Are you a danger junkie or are you just unaware of your own safety?"

The familiar voice made her heart skip a beat. "Are you planning to put me in danger again?" she asked, wondering where the Jaguar driver was hiding.

Only a few feet from where she stood, he stepped out of the shadows and stopped in a swath of light cast through one of the high windows. Though she wanted to move away from him, she kept her ground. She could see him clearly now, all six-foot-plus of him, taut muscle molded beneath a finely woven cotton shirt with sleeves rolled up to his elbows. No sunglasses to hide his thick-lashed green eyes or the rugged expanse of cheekbones that defined him. He wasn't handsome so much as he was mesmerizing.

"This wing was closed off for a reason," he said.

A bit tense, she gazed around at the dusty furniture. "Ghosts?"

"Could be."

Her pulse beat against her throat. "I don't believe in ghosts."

"Well, believe this wing is dangerous and stay out of here, Melanie."

Startled, she asked, "You know who I am? You're not some relative I haven't met yet?"

"We're not related...and you look like Olivia."

"You knew my mother?"

"I did. You have my condolences."

The first words from him that gave her pause. His inflection, too. Touched that a tall tale invented by her mother made him sound sad, Melanie softened toward him just a bit.

"News travels fast," she murmured. "I mean, Grandfather's private investigator only just learned about her death."

"There are a lot of interested ears and loose lips on an estate this size."

"You live here then?"

"Not anymore. Not since before you were born."

More to pique her interest. Who was he? In what capacity had he lived on the estate?

"My father worked here. My grandfather before him."

He was quite a bit older than she, but Melanie was lousy at guessing ages. He could be her mother's age for all she knew. Often mistaken for her older sister, her mother looked far younger than forty-three.

As did he.

"So who are you?" she asked, trying to sound more self-possessed than she was feeling.

"A restoration architect by profession. I'm going to bring this wing back to life. Ross Bennet."

He held out his hand. Melanie hesitated only a second before taking it.

"Melanie Pierce."

His flesh was warm and pulsed against hers. Again a feeling of familiarity struck her—as if she already knew Ross. Well, in a manner of speaking she did, if she considered the almost-accident on the road. Disturbed by the unexpected connection—normally she wasn't attracted to older men, who were usually too unimaginative for her taste—Melanie quickly pulled her hand free and stepped farther into the dusty room to cover.

"So what was this area used for? It's so…well, huge!"

"Ballrooms needed to be huge."

"A ballroom." She twirled a few times, imagining the strains of music. "I've never been in a house with a ballroom before."

"There's a first time for everything."

"So I've discovered."

First time. Only why didn't it feel like a first time? Why did everything seem so familiar?

She looked up and saw a ragged tear in the ceiling above, as if something had been ripped from it.

"You might want to move away from there," Ross said.

"Why? Afraid I'll be covered in crumbling plaster or something?"

"Or something," he said.

Not wanting to argue about it, she ambled back toward him, saying, "I still can't believe Mom never told me about her family."

Though she hoped his response would give her some clue to the past, he didn't take her opening. All he said was, "Slater House must have come as some surprise to you."

"Not part of my reality."

"You'll get used to it."

Before she could stop the words from coming, "I'm not sure I want to" was out of her mouth.

What was she thinking, saying something so revealing to a stranger?

"You have a problem learning you're wealthy?" he asked. "For some people, that would be a dream come true."

"Being able to make films that speak to the heart and that inspire change is *my* dream. Besides, my grandfather has money, not me."

"It's family wealth. You're family now."

"True." That was her *purpose* here, she reminded herself. To find family now that her mother was assumed dead. She'd best not argue the point. "It's just all so weird to me…going from not knowing I had another relative in the world to…this."

"You could sound more thrilled."

"I want to be thrilled. Maybe I will be. Give me some time to absorb it all. To get used to the people."

"Frederick can be difficult," Ross said. "But to him, family is everything."

"I wouldn't know." She watched him carefully when she said, "Obviously my mother had some reason for leaving and never telling me about my roots."

But Ross remained straight-faced when he said, "Sometimes your grandfather expects too much of the people he loves."

"Is that a warning?"

"Call it an observation."

If Ross knew anything concrete, he wasn't forth-coming so Melanie decided to drop it for now. Push-ing at him for too many answers at once might make him question her motives for being here. As far as he was concerned, she was the newly found grand-daughter seeking her family roots.

Changing the subject, she asked, "So why do you think I'm a danger junkie?"

"Not many people would simply walk into such an inhospitable environment."

"It's deserted and dusty, but it didn't look partic-ularly dangerous."

She thought he was going to say something but the moment passed and he backed off.

He shrugged. "I've just started inspecting the wing myself to identify any safety issues."

"So you'll let me know if you find anything?"

"If I see you around, I'll be happy to keep you informed."

He sounded amused now, at her expense. Irritated, Melanie gave him a bored sigh and said, "Anything to keep a Slater happy, eh?"

His smile faded and she swept by him, head held high. But by the time she walked into the sunlight, the moment's triumph waned. She enjoyed sparring with him—he wasn't dull no matter that he was at least ten years older than she—but she'd liked it better when they'd gotten along for those few minutes.

She continued her tour of the property, circling

around to the front of the house, passing a pathway edged by an azalea bush with orange-red flowers so brilliant they looked to be on fire. She stopped for a moment, her gaze following the meandering path to a seating area surrounded by more azaleas of various shades—lavender and peach and magenta—and she wished she'd brought her camcorder.

Later, she thought. She would record every detail of the estate. Digital memories were better than nothing.

Would her mother want to see them? she wondered, approaching the door that would lead her into the library. The door was open, the library awaiting her before she stopped short, heart pumping.

How had she known where that door would lead? She hadn't been able to see the library earlier, but she'd been certain it was here…almost like a memory.

"Can I help you, miss?" a maid asked. One of the maids who'd been upstairs earlier.

Melanie figured they'd finished with her floor—she could get into her mother's old quarters.

"Thanks, but I'm just taking my grandfather's advice and exploring. Don't pay me any mind."

"Of course, miss."

Melanie took in the walls of books. The library was on two levels, with a spiral staircase ascending to a walkway along the upper level. She'd never seen so many books in a private collection. Then again, she'd never before seen what could be called a private collection of any sort. She had a lot of books, as did most of her friends, but hers were stacked on bookcases wherever she'd found an available nook. But to think of having a whole library of one's own...

Everything at Slater House was meant to be in excess, she told herself. Undoubtedly the books were for show. She doubted anyone even used this room other than to sit by the fireplace, brandy in hand.

About to tell the maid she was done exploring here, Melanie realized the young woman had already left. Following suit, she hurried out of the room, down the hall and across the foyer, then down another hall to the staircase that would take her to her quarters.

And to her mother's past.

The upstairs hallway was clear. Melanie trod lightly over an Oriental runner, barely glancing at the artwork decorating the walls. Barely noticing the hallway that led into the north wing. Her gaze was glued to the door ahead.

A door that proved to be locked!

Now, that didn't make any sense. If the maids cleaned the room, it should be open. Well, the staff obviously had access to the key. She could just pick up a telephone and call Johnson and ask to be let in.

Something kept her from it.

Something made her check the door to the adjoining quarters. Open. And from the looks of the entry room, no sign of occupancy. She moved through the sitting room to the terrace doors, these on the side of the main building rather than facing the back gardens. Deserted. She slid out of the room and moved to a second set of terrace doors—the ones to the Buttercup Suite.

Locked.

Now what?

Melanie stared at the doors as if they would magically open, which of course they didn't. An image suddenly flashed through her mind and she turned her gaze downward to the limestone block half hidden by a stone container erupting with blue and red and gold flowers.

Heart thumping, she knelt and touched the block… which shifted slightly when she pressed one end. The block easily came out in her hand. She reached inside the opening and pulled out a single key.

Scary, she thought, staring at it.

How had she known the key was there?

As if she remembered…again….

This kind of thing had happened to her more than once before at home. The first incident she remembered, she'd been a little kid and Mom had mentioned her baby book, something her mother had put together before she was born. Melanie hadn't wanted to wait for her mother to show it to her. Even though Mom hadn't told her where to find it, she'd gone straight to the correct shelf and straight to the right book.

Several things like that had happened to her…always connected to her mother.

Melanie replaced the loose block, then used the key to let herself inside the room. The scent of lilies immediately enveloped her. One of her mother's favorite flowers. There they were on a freestanding table to one side of the sitting room—orange and yellow lilies that complemented the rest of the brightly colored space. It wasn't called the Buttercup Suite for nothing.

This was the cheeriest, least conservative room she'd seen so far. The room most likely to appeal to her. But her mother? Her mother was the Rose Suite, classic and subdued....

Apparently she hadn't always been that way.

The walls were yellow. Not a pale, vapid yellow, but a brilliant shade that made Melanie feel at home. The upholstery was flowered—sprays of buttercups on fields of dark green leaves. The few pieces of art on the walls were modern and mismatched and equally compelling.

Melanie wandered into the bedroom, where the spreads and drapes matched the upholstery in the sitting room. One dresser held a graduation photo— she found her mother immediately and realized why no one had any trouble identifying her as Olivia's daughter. Her mother's hair had been pulled back into some kind of twist—not magenta-streaked, perhaps, but close enough in style to the way Melanie wore her hair now.

It was like looking at herself in another time frame.

What set Melanie's pulse to fluttering was the fact that the faces surrounding her mother's seemed somehow familiar to her, as well.

"You're really going to see him?"

The voice came out of nowhere.

Melanie jumped and whipped around to see who was standing behind her...no one!

Suddenly woozy, she clutched a chair back for

support. Even as she tried to get her bearings, she felt as if she were floating....

"OLIVIA! Tell me!"

"Wouldn't you see him if you could?" I ask, throwing my hard hat and riding crop on a chair.

I just came in from a ride and he was there, at the stables. I'm still tingling with excitement.

"That's different and you know it," Jannie says as she stares at her reflection in my bedroom mirror. "We're of the same class."

A pretty eighteen-year-old with pale blue eyes and light brown hair pulled back in a bouncy ponytail, Jannie is tugging at the neckline of her maid's uniform, as if lowering it a bit will make it more attractive. Only a few months older than I am, Jannie has always lived here, just as I have. Through the years we've built a friendship that tests the servant-family pecking order.

"I see people for who they are," I say. "Isn't that the way it should be?"

She faces me, scowling. "You know your father will have a cow, Olivia."

Though my stomach tightens at the thought of his disapproval, I airily say, "My father would never be so common as to have a cow."

I sigh and plunk down on the bed where I struggle to remove my riding boots. That's what the mudroom is for, I know.

Father will have a fit if he sees me tracking stable muck through the house. But I don't care. One of the small defiances I allow myself as he has become so overprotective of me since Mama's death.

The defiances are becoming more frequent, my newest my plans for this evening. A thought that sends my pulse rushing crazily through every part of me.

I glance at my friend, who still looks worried for me.

"Oh, stop, please," I beg. "What's the worst that could happen?"

"You don't seriously want to go there...."

MELANIE BLINKED and gasped, then looked around dazedly for the maid. She was still alone in the room.

What the hell had just happened? she wondered, feeling a little spooked.

A memory?

Her mother's?

She'd certainly felt as if she'd been out of her own skin—thinking someone else's thoughts, saying her words, and the maid had called her Olivia.

What she'd just seen and heard had been as clear as any video, blasting her in vivid color and detail.

But how...?

She and her mother had always had a connection—and those small incidents that now seemed like memories—but this experience was new and startling, played out in Technicolor and stereo sound.

Almost as if she were reliving her mother's past.

Chapter Four

Properly spooked, her heart thumping madly, Melanie left her mother's quarters the way she'd come, making sure to lock the door behind her. She stood there for a moment to catch her breath and let her head clear.

Her imagination had gotten the better of her. That was all it had been.

Still…the experience had seemed so very real….

Shaking herself out of it, Melanie wondered if she should replace the key. In the end, she decided not to. This had been her mother's secret—one of her so-called defiances—and undoubtedly no one else knew about it.

Realizing she'd just given credence to what she'd imagined inside the suite, Melanie squeezed the key so hard it bit into her hand.

"Stop it, Melanie," she muttered to herself. "Just breathe and get a hold of yourself."

She was slipping the key into her pocket when a horse's excited whinny caught her attention. Johnson had said Mom liked to study with a view of the horses being exercised outside the stables.

No wonder Mom had seemed so horse crazy. She'd made sure Melanie had taken riding lessons before she'd started school. For years they'd driven out to the suburbs where they'd ridden on the Forest Preserve trails using rented horses. And when Mom had made her first killing in real estate, she'd talked about buying her own horse, but then had given it up—she'd decided the limited time she had to exercise the horse would be unfair to the animal.

The pounding of hooves and a series of snorts made Melanie move to the rail—there was an exercise yard and a hilly fenced area beyond, where several jumps were set up.

An older man she hadn't seen before in full riding dress was easily taking a bay over the jumps. He seemed so at ease that he might have been born in a saddle. Definitely not hired help. Well, not unless he was a riding master, which she supposed he could be.

He made the last jump with inches to spare, then sat back in the saddle as the horse circled the field. When mount and rider were nearly square with her, the rider looked up. He saw her, she was certain, for as the horse continued to circle, the man's gaze stayed glued in her direction.

Feeling somehow naked—caught where she probably shouldn't be—Melanie backed up, out of sight. She took a steadying breath and told herself no one could tell she'd been in her mother's quarters, which were at one end of the terrace. Several other rooms opened onto it, and there were stairs leading down to a lower terrace and then to the area in back of the stables.

She could almost see herself shooting down the stairs on the way for a ride....

Okay, now she was freaking herself out.

Melanie backtracked to the Rose Suite. After securing the key in a small zippered compartment of her camera pouch, she unpacked the few things she'd brought and then took a long soak in the deep claw-footed tub. She needed to get herself together, to have her wits about her, so she could be at her best when she faced her relatives once more.

The scented hot water relaxed her and by the time she got out of the tub, she was ready to face anything, even her grandfather, even if she wouldn't be properly dressed for dinner. She was who she was and he would have to accept her as such.

Slipping into black sateen crop pants, a black lace-edged camisole and sheer mesh shrug, she wasn't sure of anything, least of all her ability to delve into a past that had driven her mother from this place.

While Mom had done well in the real estate business for the past dozen years, Melanie remembered it hadn't always been that way. They'd had some really lean years. Tough years. Years when Mom had been going to school in addition to working at low-paying jobs.

Melanie just couldn't fathom why she'd chosen that very difficult path.

More to the point, she couldn't imagine why

now—twenty-five years later—Mom wanted her own father to believe she was dead.

Thinking about Frederick Slater made her extra-careful—conservative, for her—about her appearance. She brushed her hair back from her face and looped it smoothly in back, securing it with a large plain clip. A single thin bangle bracelet on each wrist and a pair of understated black jet shoulder-duster earrings completed the outfit. A smudge of kohl around her eyes and a dab of gloss on her lips and she was as ready as she would ever be to face her family.

Leaving her room feeling a bit shaky, Melanie almost expected to hear a ghost from the past talking to her again. The only thing she heard as she moved along the hall, though, was her own breath, quick and light. At the top of the stairs she stopped to gather herself. Voices drifted up to her. Good thing she had no expectations, for the sound wasn't warm and welcoming. More like an unhappy buzz.

Did these people never laugh?

Or was it simply that her arrival had disrupted their comfortable lives?

Tension drifted up the staircase and enveloped her, made her want to turn around and return to her room. She couldn't, of course. No point in her being here if she didn't accomplish what she'd set out to do.

Hold back, she told herself. View the scene. Wide shot moving slowly down the stairs until the lens catches up with the subjects scattered around the indoor garden room.

The light was still good. The sun might be low on

the horizon, but it hadn't yet set, and the skylights glowed above and washed the scene below with a gentle radiance. Everyone was here—her grandfather, uncle, aunts-by-marriage and a man with silver-laced blond hair that she hadn't yet met who, if she wasn't mistaken, was the horseman.

Wearing a taupe suit that fit his tall, athletic physique like a glove, he was quite impressive. His presence was unmistakable—both his straight back and confident air obviously came naturally to him and would put him in good stead on the back of a hunter-jumper.

Feeling calmer now, Melanie was able to join the others without stumbling over her own feet. Johnson was swinging through the group, his tray heavy with drinks.

"Where is the girl?" she heard her grandfather demand of the butler. "She was told to be prompt."

"And so she is," Johnson said smoothly, nodding in her direction.

All heads turned her way. Aware of not-so-subtle stares, Melanie categorized her relatives into two camps—suspicious or outright hostile—with her grandfather being the exception. As a filmmaker, she'd dealt with their types and worse before. At least her relatives weren't violent.

Melanie adopted her most dazzling smile, the one she used to put potential subjects at ease. *I'm so happy to see you,* it said. *And so glad you're considering being a part of this project.*

As he dispensed the last glass from his tray, Johnson asked, "What would you like to drink, Miss Melanie?"

"Something cool and refreshing would be wonderful."

"Sweet tea?"

"Perfect."

"We haven't yet met," the horseman said, closing in on her from one side while her grandfather approached her from the other.

"This is Andrew Lennox, my dear. Helen's brother. He's lived with her in the north wing since your uncle Nicholas left her a widow."

"I also happen to be head of your grandfather's legal team," Andrew said, offering her his hand.

Team? Most people didn't even have a lawyer but her grandfather had an entire team? She supposed with his wealth, he had use for more than one.

"I'm pleased to meet you," she murmured.

For a moment he stared so deeply into her face that it made the skin along her spine crawl.

Suddenly he seemed to realize he was making her ill at ease. "Forgive me. I don't mean to make you uncomfortable. But, my word, the resemblance…"

"So you knew my mother."

He nodded. "Olivia was a charming young woman."

His tone told her he'd held her mother in high regard. Melanie relaxed and smiled at him.

He continued. "If I didn't know better…"

"Here you go, miss," Johnson said, holding out a tall glass.

"Thank you." Melanie held up the glass as if in a toast to her grandfather and Andrew, and took a sip. Saying it was sweet tea was no exaggeration.

The butler whispered something into her grand-father's ear and the next thing she knew Frederick Slater was backing away and making his excuses. "If need be," he told everyone, "start dinner without us."

Then he and Andrew headed off, away from the family gathering. Melanie got a glimpse of a third man—who saw her, as well—before they all disappeared into another room.

John Grey.

Melanie couldn't help it—unbearable tension took hold of her once more. Why was the private investigator here now? He'd seen her, too.

What would he tell her grandfather?

Before she could relax, the sound of footsteps against the stone floor alerted her of another presence.

"Melanie, this is Ross Bennet," Eleanor was saying, actually sounding as pleased as a cat licking cream. "He's here to see to some restoration. I'm sure the two of you will have a *lot* in common."

Melanie couldn't miss the inflection on "lot." So what did that mean?

"Melanie, how nice to meet you," Ross was saying, as if it were for the first time.

The next thing she knew, he tucked a hand in the small of her back and directed her away from where her relatives sat. He stopped in the middle of the room, where the fountain's splash covered whatever her relatives were now saying about her. Not that she was paranoid or anything.

"You clean up real nice," he said softly.

As did he. Not that she was going to say so. He

wore a pale gray suit with a darker gray shirt and a black tie. Not her taste, of course. He appeared as subdued as…well, as she did tonight.

She murmured, "So we haven't met before?" Did he fear her grandfather would fire him if he knew about the fiasco at the blind curve?

He shrugged. "That's up to you. Your grandfather does have certain standards when it comes to whom the family sees or befriends." His smile was charming, but she sensed tension below the surface.

"You're afraid of him." A fact that surprised her.

He gave her an offended expression. "I simply like to keep clients happy. As I said, it's up to you."

No, maybe not afraid, she amended. But something was making him extra cautious.

"All right," she agreed. "I won't breathe a word of our earlier trysts."

His smile was all teeth, like those of a predator. Melanie took a step back.

"No need to be nervous," he assured her.

"Isn't there?"

He'd gotten her to do exactly as he'd wanted. She hated being manipulated.

Ross laughed and the sound echoed up toward the skylight. The low buzz behind them stopped and Melanie realized her relatives had gone silent and speculative.

"Perhaps we should join the others," she murmured.

"Your wish…"

Was his command? She couldn't imagine him doing anything he didn't want to do.

As they approached the others, Ross was all charm. "Ladies, you're looking lovely tonight."

Helen blushed and murmured a "Thank you." But Eleanor merely rolled her eyes.

Melanie couldn't help herself. "So what's going on in there?" she said, indicating the room where the three men had sequestered themselves.

"Family business."

"*I'm* family."

"I told you she wanted in for the money," Eleanor waspishly told her husband.

Melanie straightened. "I'm in because I just learned I had relatives and was told they wanted to meet me."

"*Frederick* wanted to meet you."

No one else countered Eleanor's undoubtedly accurate remark.

"Perhaps I'll grow on you," Melanie muttered.

"I doubt it."

"Then think of me as a guest. Surely you treat *guests* with some courtesy."

"How dare you!"

Even Melanie didn't know how she dared be so defiant. It wasn't part of her plan. Normally she could hold her temper with anyone if she put her mind to it. It was this place, she thought. Slater House was unexpected and so were her reactions. Too close. She was getting too close. She needed to back off and to keep looking at these people through the distance of her director's lens.

Echoing her thoughts, Ross said, "Perhaps we all need to take a step back."

"You especially."

"Eleanor," Helen said, as if shocked at her sister-in-law's rudeness.

"Enough," Martin added, glowering at his wife for a moment before turning his attention to Ross. "Tell us about your plans for the south wing."

"Not much to tell yet. At the moment I'm gathering impressions of what it must have looked like in its glory. And I'm taking notes on safety issues, of course. The roof isn't good and there are other structural things that need to be taken care of. Right now, that's my priority."

Melanie noted that Helen clasped her hands together tightly in her lap. The woman was staring down at them as if she couldn't bear to glance at Ross, who went on smoothly, as if nothing had happened to disturb her.

He could be quite the charmer, when he chose.

Or a con man.

For a moment Melanie indulged herself and viewed the scene as she would if she were shooting a movie. Ross doing his best to con the others... though to what point, she couldn't yet discern—he reminded her of a dark-haired Paul Newman in *The Sting.* Uncle Martin simmering down and pretending to be congenial. Eleanor studying Ross as if she were trying to read him. And Helen remaining altogether withdrawn from the conversation.

What a cast of characters!

Before she could consider a movie premise, Johnson announced, "Dinner is served."

The butler stood in the doorway of a room Melanie hadn't yet seen.

"Frederick is still in a meeting," Eleanor informed him. "Cook will have to hold dinner."

"She'll have to do no such thing." Frederick's voice boomed across the expanse as he rejoined the group, Andrew following. "It seems as if our timing is perfect."

He strode past the butler and stopped to inspect Melanie. "Yes, much better. Now you look like her."

Before Melanie knew what he was about, her grandfather stooped and kissed her cheek. Uncomfortable at the show of affection from a man she didn't know and wasn't sure she should like, she took a step back. She couldn't miss his expression— annoyance and suppressed anger.

He quickly covered, though, smoothing his features before guiding her to the table.

Everyone rose and followed to preassigned seats. Melanie found herself at the foot of the table, opposite her grandfather, with Andrew on her left and Ross on her right. An uncomfortable spot to be in considering Eleanor was shooting daggers at her. Melanie wondered if this was Eleanor's usual place at the table. She probably thought of herself as the mistress of the house. Tempted to ask if she wanted to trade places, Melanie held her tongue.

She didn't have to be liked, she reminded herself. She hadn't expected it, hadn't expected to like the people who were her family, not with her mother on the run and all. Nothing else should matter, though of course it did. She wasn't used to being disliked just for being who she was. She was merely here to find the truth about the past.

Her grandfather didn't seem out of sorts or anything, Melanie thought, so perhaps Grey hadn't told him anything new, such as the truth about her mother being alive. But how could she be sure his P.I. hadn't betrayed Mom? No use in dwelling on it now. She needed a clear mind to get through this meal and perhaps learn something she needed to know.

For a moment she concentrated on the room itself.

The dining room's walls rose twelve feet high, the lower four feet of marble wainscoting. The centerpiece of the room was the tile-trimmed fireplace. The damask linen-covered dining table sat next to it. Melanie didn't think she'd ever seen such a display of china and silver and crystal. The room lights were dim, but both table and fireplace mantel were heavy with lit candles.

Johnson oversaw two maids who handled the food, starting with cream of asparagus soup ladled from a silver tureen at the table. Maids…*Jannie*… Was there really a Jannie in the house? she wondered as the butler filled her goblet with Merlot wine from a bottle with the Slater Vineyards label.

Before anyone could start eating, Frederick made a toast. "To my granddaughter taking her rightful place in my home and at my table."

"To Melanie," Ross agreed, his voice smoothing out some of the rockiness she was feeling.

"To Slater House and its future," she toasted in return.

Eleanor snorted and downed her wine without further comment.

And Melanie found herself doing the same. If she said everything she wanted, she would never get anything of value from these people.

Then she would have no idea of how to protect her mother.

Chapter Five

Dinner proved to be as uncomfortable as Ross had imagined, but not for him. Despite Frederick's hold on the family, Melanie was shut out of conversation, vividly by Eleanor, more subtly by Martin and vaguely by Helen. He could see the tension in the straightness of her spine, in the way she held her fork. Somehow she managed to keep her thoughts to herself, to hold her own without seeming petty herself.

So much like Olivia.

Maybe that was why, despite a rocky beginning, he was so drawn to her.

"I understand you direct films," he said.

"Documentaries."

"Sounds challenging."

"One of the reasons I love what I do." Her eyes lit, so they shone in a room full of darkness. "I pity the person who can't learn from his or her work. Something new every day keeps me stimulated."

Indeed, her face flushed becomingly with color as she went on to talk about her work. A film about children from various countries exploring their native heritages while integrating into the American culture. Another about teenage girls making choices about dating and relationships. A third about zoo curators and their personal attachments to the animals they protected.

"You're very accomplished for one so young," Andrew said.

"I graduated from college ahead of my contemporaries, and I've been on the fast track ever since."

"Nothing wrong with that," Ross said, appreciating the fact that she was on her way to an incredible career and she'd done it on her own.

The way he had.

"Soon you'll be too busy for your little films," Frederick said.

Melanie stopped her fork halfway to her mouth. "Busy doing what?"

"Being a Slater, of course."

"There's no 'of course' about it," Melanie said, her voice tight as she dropped the fork on her plate. "A filmmaker is who I am. That's not going to change."

Whatever Frederick wanted to say, he swallowed it and took another sip of his wine.

Ross feigned picking up something from the ground between him and Melanie and murmured, "Good for you," for her ears only.

So she would continue working on documentaries. Frederick would come around. And he would throw money at her, instruct her to make documentaries of more consequence. She wouldn't have to struggle for long. She would soon have everything she'd ever wanted…not to mention things she hadn't even known she wanted.

Frederick would see to it.

Soon, Melanie Pierce Slater—Ross was certain the old man would insist she legally change her name—would be able to do whatever she wanted, whenever she wanted.

And wouldn't it be interesting if she turned to him, of all people, Ross thought, to help her make those decisions?

"I'm going to give a party in your honor," Frederick suddenly announced, his attention fully on his granddaughter.

"A party…why?"

"To introduce you to North Carolina society, of course. Not a big event. Eleanor, you make up an invitation list. Keep it intimate, perhaps a hundred or so."

Eleanor looked ready to choke but she wisely kept her counsel.

"I won't be here that long," Melanie protested.

"Of course you will. The party will be on Saturday."

Only a few days away. Still she said, "I don't know—"

"But I do," Frederick cut in, his voice sharp with icy resolve. "Don't worry your pretty head about the details. You won't have to do anything. A consultant will see to your person. And I shall give you a choice of several escorts I deem suitable."

Tension radiated from Melanie. Though Ross figured no one could miss it, no one commented, not even the subject of the old man's manipulation. Melanie finished her meal, stiff-faced, quickly.

And then before dessert was served, she stood, saying, "If you'll excuse me, I have a headache and need some fresh air." Without waiting for her grandfather's approval, she made directly for the terrace doors.

The expressions around the table ranged from shocked to outright anger. The last being Frederick, of course. He could never stand being foiled.

As Ross watched Melanie's dignified retreat, he smiled and decided that it would be in his best interests to be her escort when she was introduced to proper North Carolina society.

TRYING TO EASE her anger, Melanie walked through the gardens and around the stables toward the front of the house only to spot John Grey leaving the building by one of the minor entrances—the one, she assumed, to her grandfather's study.

"Mr. Grey!" she called sharply. "You have some questions to answer."

The private investigator whirled around to face her as she stepped between him and the parked cars in the drive. There was a weird chill to the night that put her even more on edge than she already was.

"What is it, Miss Slater?"

"The name is Pierce, as you well know."

"Not for long."

She ignored her instinct to fight him on that one. "I need to know what you told my grandfather."

"I'm sorry, but our business is private."

"Not if it concerns me or my mother," she said, wanting reassurance that he hadn't spilled the beans.

Grey's smile was twisted and his raspy voice lowered when he said, "Why, your mother is *dead*... right?"

The way he said it put fear in her, almost making her believe that Mom *was* dead. But of course he was playing a part. A convincing one, she thought, noting the threads of fog that rose from the ground, crawling up his legs as if he were the Grim Reaper himself.

"My mother is to stay dead for as long as she needs to. Are we clear on that?"

"You're threatening me?" Grey asked incredulously. "I stay silent...or you'll what?"

Melanie's pulse surged at the private investigator's nasty tone. She had only one card to play.

"I know about the bribe," she informed him. "My mother paid you well to protect her. If you tell *anyone* the truth, I'll inform Grandfather about your duplicity. You know him better than I. He'll ruin you."

Grey laughed, the sound raising the short hairs at the base of her neck.

"Nice try," he said when he got himself under control. "But that'll never happen, because I know *all* the secrets of Slater House."

Whatever *that* meant.

Before she could ask, he cut through the mist and slid into his car, where he quickly started the engine.

And laughed some more.

Though the windows of his car were up, Melanie

could hear the sound through the glass. As he sped away, his car was swallowed whole by fog.

Melanie tried to rub the chill from her arms. Unnerved, she felt at loose ends. Though she wished she could get into her rental car and drive off to anywhere, that was impossible. Both her car keys and her driver's license were up in her room, and she simply couldn't go back into the house just yet.

What to do?

A horse's neigh settled it for her. She headed through the rising mist for the stables.

An older man she'd not seen before poked his head out from a room in back. "Can I help you, miss? You're not wanting to ride this late, are you?"

She heard the note of disapproval in his voice.

"No, I was just out for a walk and simply wanted to visit the horses."

"Go ahead, then. You need anything, I'll be in the feed room."

All Melanie needed was a little comfort, something she'd always been able to get around horses. She loved watching them, talking to them, running her hand along their velvet noses and up between their eyes. The human-animal connection soothed her, calmed her down a bit. The horses demanded nothing from her, had no criticism. They simply enjoyed her company as she enjoyed theirs.

Sometime later, aware of a car engine starting, she went to the door and looked out across the courtyard as the red Jaguar circled around and cut through the fog toward the road that would take its driver off the property. Ross was leaving, so the gathering inside must have broken up.

Ross....

Melanie wondered where he lived. How he lived. What he did with his time when he wasn't working.

An aggravating man...but interesting...and definitely attractive.

Not that she had time to do anything about it other than notice. She wouldn't be here long enough to worry about anything other than finding the truth so she could protect her mother.

Saying good-night to the horses, she headed across the courtyard. The house glowed eerily, the moon adding a supernatural glow to the haze that clung to the stone. Like something out of *The Shining,* she thought. She slipped inside the front door.

She heard the low murmur of voices as the staff shut down the house for the night—outside doors locked, lights shut off or lowered.

Melanie waited for several minutes until all was quiet and her eyes adjusted to the dark. Then she began moving freely through the house, guided by instincts more than by an occasional night-light or the paltry bits of moonlight that filtered through the high windows.

The first-floor rooms were all huge, high-ceilinged and chilly at night. Melanie didn't really know what she was doing exploring them now. Sleep was the last thing on her mind, though, and she thought she might go crazy if she went back to her rooms simply to lie awake and stare into the dark.

She couldn't forget what had happened in Mom's old quarters, either.

Would there be more?

Melanie moved down the hall, wending her way through room after room as if she knew their nooks and crannies. Why did everything seem so familiar? The walls seemed to talk to her, whispering their welcome home.

And they seemed to have eyes…all on her.

Was someone there in the dark watching her? she wondered, her heart beginning to pound.

Or was her imagination simply out of whack?

Whatever….

Swearing she heard the scrape of a shoe from somewhere—the acoustics were so bad in this area she had no sense of direction—Melanie did an about-face and moved back the way she had come. Her pulse fluttered and her mouth had gone dry. She was trying not to breathe so that she could hear if there were more footsteps.

Part of her was ready for a jump—someone stepping out of the woodwork to confront her. Part of her simply wanted to get to the safety of her room.

Assuming it was safe.

Finding the stairs, she practically ran up them, throwing a look over her shoulder only once when halfway up. Was that a movement in the shadows? She forced her feet to move so fast that she barely skimmed each stair, nearly flew up the last quarter of the staircase.

When she reached the landing, she ran to her

quarters, threw open the door, then slammed and locked it before resting her back against the wooden panel.

Her imagination.

Had to be.

Otherwise she was already in trouble.

MELANIE'S PRESENCE chilled him—she looked so much like her mother. He'd hoped Olivia was really dead, but of course she wasn't.

Some things were better left unsaid.

Some women were better left dead.

He laughed at the rhyme. And at Olivia's fate.

Not that he was amused. He was angry. Furious, actually. He hated being thwarted when he had a goal.

Good thing he hadn't trusted John Grey. He'd waited until the middle of the night to check things out for himself. The P.I.'s Slater Corners office had been easy to get into—Slater Corporation owned the building, after all, and the keys were easily enough accessible.

The folder he'd found in Grey's desk had laid it all out for him—a veritable dossier on Olivia Pierce. Details about her personal life. More about her business, including a big deal she'd brokered just a few months before.

Interesting that she'd sold a commercial building more than a year after her supposed fatal car accident.

Interesting that Melanie hadn't denied the claim that Olivia had passed on.

What was Melanie up to?

Not that it mattered in the long run. The bitch

would have her turn. No doubt she simply wanted her share of the Slater fortune, and it would be his pleasure to make sure she, too, was dead before she could get her hands on it.

But first he would see to Olivia, he thought, his mood darkening further. If only he could get his hands on her right now....

He was copying down her Chicago address when the door opened.

Caught!

A red haze skewed his vision.

"What the hell are *you* doing in here?" a bug-eyed John Grey demanded.

"Checking on you. Learning that you're a liar and a cheat."

"I should have you arrested for breaking and entering."

The threat brought him to his feet. He couldn't have that. Couldn't have anyone knowing. If anyone put two and two together...

"You're not going to tell anyone."

"Then you're going to keep the secret?" Grey asked.

"The secret? Oh, yes. Definitely."

He grabbed Grey by the throat. The private investigator flailed. Couldn't have that. He turned the P.I. and aimed his head at the cabinets. At the first strike, Grey's eyes rolled back, but one strike wasn't enough. He smashed his head over and over until it was bloody pulp and the bastard sank to the floor. Then he kicked and kicked and kicked until the anger drained out of him.

Breathing hard, he stooped to feel for a nonexistent pulse.

Good. He smiled.

And then turned back to the dossier on Olivia, removed the recent reference to her and replaced the folder where he'd found it. Good thing he'd worn gloves. No fingerprints. He was always careful to cover his back.

Rummaging through the cabinets, he stopped when he came across a folder of a local criminal and dropped it on the floor so that it was half hidden by the desk. Hopefully, there. That would send the police in the wrong direction.

Smiling now, he stuffed the information about Olivia into a pocket—he didn't want anyone else finding it and coming to the same conclusion he had—and let himself out of the office. A quick look around assured him the street was deserted. Pulling his billed cap low over his eyes, he walked several blocks to where he'd left his car.

And all the while thoughts of Olivia crowded out anything else from his mind.

Now that she'd been found, he would make certain she died for real.

Chapter Six

The smell of fresh hay in the stables was comfortingly familiar as Melanie crossed the courtyard from the house. Breakfast would be served buffet style between seven and eight. Having risen early as usual, she had an hour to kill. With no one to talk to in the house, she decided to pay the horses another visit.

The stalls were already mucked and the horses already fed. She stopped to pat a chestnut munching on some oats.

"A mount for you, miss?" asked a stablehand. "Name's Billy, by the way."

Approaching middle age, Billy had the wiry body of a man who worked off his food with hard labor and the leather face of one who spent too many hours in the sun.

Tempted, she reminded herself of her purpose here—certainly not to indulge herself. "Thank you, Billy, but not this morning. Perhaps later. Or tomorrow."

"Very good, miss. Say the word and we'll find a proper mount for you."

Interesting that he didn't even bother to ask if she knew how to ride. Apparently he assumed anyone who visited Slater House did. And perhaps he was correct.

Melanie speculated that riding out with one of her relatives might be common ground on which she could get close enough to dig for information.

Oh, who was she kidding? The grasping Eleanor would never deign to ride with her. Helen seemed too introverted to ride at all. And Martin…

Before she could finish the thought, she heard horses coming in and her grandfather's voice.

"Billy, over here. Sir Galahad needs a cool-down. Delaware Bay, also."

Having wandered down the aisle, checking out the horses in their stalls, Melanie saw her grandfather and Andrew dismount from a gray and a bay respectively. Billy took both horses into the courtyard where he hand-walked them. She thought to call out to the men to let them know she was here, but considering she was still angry with her grandfather, she changed her mind.

Instinctively she stepped into an empty stall—she could see them both through the boards, but they couldn't see her.

Her grandfather said, "The only proper way to start the day is on the back of a horse."

"You do know how to live, Frederick. So many men allow time to slow them down. Not you."

"And why should I let it? Exercise has kept me young. My doctor says I have the heart of a man twenty years my junior."

"At this rate, you'll live to be a hundred!"

Her grandfather laughed and led the way out of the stables. "Perhaps I shall."

The heart of a man twenty years younger? Live to be a hundred? Those didn't sound like the words of a man who was ill, Melanie thought, leaving the shelter of the empty stall. John Grey had told her that Frederick Slater was ill and had indicated he wanted to meet her before it was too late.

More manipulation!

Melanie took a deep, calming breath. She hadn't gotten over her grandfather's assumptions at dinner the night before—that she would soon quit making her little films, that she would allow someone to dress her properly for this intended party that she had no interest in and that she would allow him to pick potential escorts for her.

Melanie clenched her jaw in irritation. Mostly she was irritated with herself, for she knew she would let her grandfather think he was swaying her at least enough to appease him. How else was she going to learn what she had come to North Carolina to find out?

Waiting only long enough to make certain the men didn't see her coming from the stables, Melanie set out for the house and the breakfast room, yet another example of Slater House excess. In addition to the dining room and breakfast room, apparently there was also a banquet room, which would be used for the party in her honor.

If she stayed that long.

Then again, the party might even be a good idea. Surely among the cream of North Carolina society, there would be a few people who'd known her mother.

Hoping to get her key to the past more quickly, Melanie figured she might better be able to obtain it from the servants. Rather, one particular servant if she really existed in more than Melanie's imagination.

She entered the breakfast room just as a maid placed a rectangular pan—half potatoes, half grits— in a warming unit. Nearby, Johnson was checking the silverware at a round table set with six places. There had been seven the night before. So who was left out?

Ross, no doubt.

She bit back her disappointment—he'd been the only bright spot in a dismal evening—and approached the table as a second maid brought in a pan of breakfast meats. "Mmm, everything smells wonderful."

"Applewood bacon. And Cook does amazing things with breakfast potatoes," the butler added.

"My mouth is already watering."

"Only a few minutes to go, miss. Mr. Frederick is always punctual."

Trying to curb her sarcastic tone, Melanie murmured, "Yes, he must have a *healthy* appetite after a morning ride."

Johnson murmured a response and set a bowl of fresh flowers in the middle of the table.

"There seems to be quite a large staff on the estate," Melanie ventured.

"It used to be much larger. Now only a handful live in the house or the old coach house. The others merely come in for the day."

"You've worked here for…?"

"Forever, miss."

"What about the others? Is everyone as loyal as you?"

"Some."

"What about a maid named Jannie?"

His eyebrows shot up. "Jannie?"

"Mom talked about her." Melanie hoped she wasn't making a fool of herself bringing up someone who might not even exist. "Apparently they were the same age, so they were friendly. Her name was Jannie, right?"

"Janine Marsh, that was her legal name."

The mental breath she'd been holding whooshed right out of her. Jannie *did* exist. It hadn't been her imagination.

"Janine hasn't worked here for more than two decades," Johnson was saying.

Forcing herself to stay focused rather than dwell on the weird incident in her mother's old quarters, Melanie asked, "She quit?"

"Mr. Frederick had to let her go. For disloyalty, unfortunately."

Two decades or twenty-five years? Disloyalty? Did that mean Jannie had something to do with her mother's disappearing act?

Hearing the clatter of feet nearby, Melanie realized her private talk with Johnson was at an end.

Still, she took advantage of the last moment they had alone to ask, "Do you know where I can find her?"

"I believe she works at a women's boutique in Slater Corners."

Slater Corners hadn't seemed that large when she'd driven through it. Melanie was certain that if Janine Marsh actually worked there, she would find her. But for the moment, she cleared her mind of the inexplicable event.

Breakfast was thankfully uneventful.

It was afterward when her grandfather and uncle Martin and Andrew left the table to do business and the women lingered over coffee that it happened.

All Melanie asked was, "So when do I get to meet my cousins? Do any of them live here?"

"Horrible girl!" Helen wailed, knocking over her chair as she rushed to get away from the table.

"What did I say? I'm sorry!"

But Helen had dashed out of the room without a glance backward.

"Aren't you just like your mother," Eleanor said caustically. "Unthinking and cruel."

"I don't understand."

Eleanor flicked her a poisonous glare and swept out of the room through the terrace doors, leaving Melanie not only confused, but upset. She'd obviously hurt Helen and didn't know why.

BACK IN HER ROOM, Melanie put the incident out of mind as she changed into low-rise jeans, a T-shirt printed with the poster of one of her films and a pair of orange sneakers.

She planned to go exploring.

First wanting to check in so her mother wouldn't be suspicious, she hit the number to Mom's cell but got her voice mail instead.

"Hey, Mom, sorry I missed you," though maybe it was best this way. Her mother wouldn't have a clue that she wasn't back in Chicago. "I think I have all the footage I need for the film. Now I have to do editing notes, see what I really do have. I guess you must be working. Good luck with that new client. Love you. Later."

A typical message. Mom would never be the wiser. Trying not to feel guilty at the deception, Melanie told herself it was for her mother's own good and set off on her exploration of the grounds.

Taking the terrace exit, she set on a wood chip path and meandered through what seemed to be a maze of hedges and trees with various choices as to the direction she would take. She could hear a burbling fountain and eventually made her way to the clearing.

The gardens were a joy to explore, but the pull of the south wing was too strong to resist. Or maybe it was the hope of seeing Ross for a few minutes.

Melanie guessed she really was a danger junkie—undoubtedly she would be wise to stay away from both.

Still…

The red Jaguar sat parked in front of a different door than the day before. An open door. She stood in the doorway for a moment, attempting to orient herself and get acclimated to the dim light inside. The ballroom sat to the left, taking up more than half of the wing's first floor.

"Ross?" she called, expecting the man to pop out of nowhere again.

Her pulse trilled as she waited in vain. And then curiosity got the best of her and she moved to the other side of the foyer.

This obviously had been a parlor. The room might be dingy now, and one wall needed repair, but the high ceiling and tall windows and marble-trimmed fireplace boded well for a stunning restoration.

Melanie moved to the next room, a game room if the dust-covered billiards table was any indication. This room looked solid enough. Wondering if the chess table was still here, she looked to the windows and started for the inlaid wood table.

Stopping before she quite reached it, her pulse beat rapidly as she realized she'd somehow *known* that there had been a chess table....

Another step and her foot landed on something that threatened to send her flying. She caught herself and looked down. On the floor, a lone chess piece stared up her. She stooped and with stiff fingers picked it up.

"I can teach you to play, if you want."

Melanie gripped the piece hard and got to her feet. "Ross? Where are you?"

He wasn't here. No one was. As the room shifted and the dust disappeared, Melanie swayed and caught herself on the edge of the table.

"WHERE DID YOU learn to play?" I ask, keeping my focus on the queen. Now that we're together, the butterflies in my stomach keep me from looking at him.

"Pop taught me."

"Your father plays?"

"Just because he doesn't have a lot of money doesn't mean he doesn't have a brain."

"I—I didn't mean that," I say, wanting to bite my tongue. I've never felt so shy before, so uncertain of myself. I stare at the chess piece, a queen, but one in an antebellum costume. Father loves to collect unusual chess sets and this one was the Blue & Gray. He always chooses the Gray, I know, and he always wins. "Your father—he's always so busy, I didn't think he would have the time."

"Sometimes it takes days to finish a game, but that's okay, because it gives us time to think out our moves."

Days…spending days with him is something I can look forward to. But I don't want to learn to play chess. I want him to teach me other things, the kinds of things that—just thinking about them—make my knees weak and my stomach flutter and my heart settle in my throat.

I whirl around to face him, boldly saying, "Kiss me, instead!"

"KISS YOU?"

Melanie jumped and blinked the room back to dustiness. Ross stood there, staring at her, his expression inscrutable.

Before she could respond, he muttered, "What-ever the lady wants," hooked a hand at her waist and pulled her to him.

Melanie opened her mouth to protest just as his lips came crashing down on hers. And then she lost her will to protest. Every nerve in her body came alive. Clutching the queen in her hand tightly, she wrapped her arms around his neck and for a moment lost herself in the kiss.

His mouth was hot. Seductive. His tongue plunged into her so boldly that her knees grew weak and she clung to him so she wouldn't fall. Her heart was pounding so hard, she was certain he could hear it.

He moaned against her mouth and her body re-sponded, insides tingling, flesh along her spine rippling.

The walls of the house seemed to whirl around her as if warning her of danger, but danger had always been an aphrodisiac to Melanie.

She lost herself to the moment….

I've never been kissed like this before. It fills me with new feelings…makes my body come alive… makes me want to do more than kiss him….

Was this real? Or imagined? The present or the past?

Confused, she shoved hard.

Ross jerked back, his expression dark, glower-ing even. Real, Melanie told herself, shocked by her own lack of inhibition. If she hadn't questioned the moment…

Gaze narrowing on the chess piece in her hand, he asked, "Where did you find that? In here?"

"On the floor." Melanie's hand was trembling and she handed it to him. Her head was warring with her body, still yearning for something more than a kiss. "The danger junkie almost took a spill."

In more ways than one.

"I tried to warn you that this was risky."

Which? The building? Or him?

"You're a man who always needs to be right, aren't you?"

His "Maybe I am always right" was enough to straighten her spine.

"So you're going to tell me I shouldn't be here."

"Why, when you already know it?"

Her lips felt stiff when she muttered, "I don't know why I thought I could talk to you."

"You wanted to talk to *me?*" He grinned at her.

"Don't flatter yourself. I simply needed to talk to someone who doesn't see me as a threat."

With that Melanie swept by Ross and out of the room. She kept going, out of the abandoned wing and onto the path toward the front of the house. This time, however, she continued onward, straight into the azalea garden.

What was she? A lunatic? Why had she gone in search of Ross? Just because he'd been charming over dinner—undoubtedly to impress the great Frederick Slater—she'd given him more credit than he deserved.

And what the heck had just happened to her? Did she really see another scene from the past? Or was her director's vision merely engaged?

She wanted to believe the second, but how could she? She'd known about the library. And the key. And the chess table.

How?

What in the world was going on?

She sank onto the bench next to the fiery azalea bush and tried to relax. But even the beauty of the garden didn't soothe her tumbling thoughts.

Her mother's memories…they had to be…but how had they been passed on to her?

Melanie didn't know how long she'd been sitting on the bench, her mind roiling with the possibilities, before she heard footsteps crunch along the gravel path. Ross—he'd come after her. Exhilarated, she looked up only to see Andrew approaching.

Telling herself she was *not* disappointed, that just because she was used to venturing into unsafe waters professionally, she didn't have to do so personally, she smiled at Andrew even while wondering why he was out here.

"Good morning," she said.

"Is it?"

Though his tone was kind, she tensed, suddenly remembering why she'd fled the house in the first place. "I assume you heard I brutalized your sister?"

"Eleanor mentioned as much."

"Eleanor…."

"Don't let her get to you. She's a self-serving bitch, only nice to those who can do something for her."

Melanie started at his words. "I thought it was

just me." She grimaced. "Helen practically went screaming from the room this morning. I was simply trying to find out more about the family by asking about any cousins."

"No wonder. May I?" he asked, indicating the bench. She nodded and he sat next to her. "Helen lost her surviving daughter last month. The ballroom. Very tragic. For some reason Louisa was exploring and the chandelier came down on top of her."

"Oh, my God!"

"Her death devastated Frederick. It's the reason he decided to restore the wing."

"So there wouldn't be any more accidents."

She remembered seeing part of the ceiling ripped out in the ballroom. No wonder Ross had called her a danger junkie. No doubt he assumed she knew.

Ross…. She glanced back at the south wing, then forced her mind away from the man.

"Wait a minute. You said 'surviving.' I take it Louisa wasn't the only child?"

"Slater children seem to carry some kind of a curse," Andrew told her, shaking his head sadly. "Over the last couple of decades, Helen and Nicholas lost a son to a riding accident. Another daughter died of crib death. Martin and Eleanor lost a daughter, too. She drowned in the stream near one of the waterfalls on the property."

"Are you saying I'm it? No, wait…isn't there a Vincent?"

"You do have one cousin. Martin and Eleanor's son. He's away on Slater Vineyards business, but he'll be back sometime today, I believe. So you and Vincent represent the future of the Slater American dynasty. You can see why Frederick sent his private investigator searching for Olivia. And why he was so delighted to find you."

"Why didn't he tell me all this himself?"

"Maybe he was afraid he'd scare you off."

"I don't scare easily."

"Good girl," Andrew said approvingly.

Melanie relaxed a little. And decided to take the opportunity to advance her private investigation. "You knew my mother, right?"

"Of course. I didn't live in the house then, but I did visit my sister and her husband often. And then I worked for Frederick, so I was here quite a lot."

"What did you think of her?"

"Olivia was bright and pretty and had such potential…just like her daughter."

"But she ran away."

"Yes."

The big question. "Why?"

"Problems between her and Frederick, I imagine. I really don't know the details."

Didn't know or wouldn't say? Did lawyer privilege apply here? Melanie wondered. Or was he simply practicing Southern restraint?

"You shouldn't dwell on the past," Andrew said. "You're not Olivia. You're your own person and you have a chance to create your own path here."

"You make a good point."

Andrew laughed. "Well, that's settled then."

"Now if only I could cancel this party in my honor."

"Changing Frederick's mind once it's made up is...um...difficult."

"You mean impossible?"

They both laughed this time.

"I have a proposition for you," Andrew said. "If you don't think me too foolish."

"And that would be?"

"To save you from Frederick's idea of a proper suitor. He'll probably scare up the dullest young Turks, any one of whom will bore you all evening. I could escort you, if you wish, and you can have as much freedom as you please."

Though Andrew was quite a bit older than she, he was charming and attractive. And he made her laugh. The offer was tempting, but...

Ross came to mind. She imagined herself in his arms, dancing.

"Melanie?"

Realizing Andrew was waiting for an answer, she flushed. "Might I think about it?"

"Not a problem, my dear. Take all the time you need. Just a suggestion. I've run out of time for my little break. Back to work for this old lawyer."

"Not so old." Midforties, she guessed. "And I'll walk with you. Oh, I need to check my e-mail. I assume there's a computer hooked up to the Internet somewhere in the house, right?"

"Several. I'll be happy to show you to one."

Andrew offered her his arm in gentlemanly fashion. In a much better mood, Melanie took it.

And then realized Ross had come out of the south wing and was staring daggers their way.

Tension filling her once more, Melanie clutched Andrew's arm and focused on the charming man while she tried to put Ross Bennet out of mind.

WHAT THE HELL was Melanie doing with Andrew Lennox?

Not liking the way his gut twisted as he watched her tuck her hand into Andrew's arm—the man was old enough to be her father—Ross tore himself from the sight and went back into the abandoned wing.

He didn't know why it bothered him. Just another attractive woman. Even as he thought it, he knew there was more to it. He'd felt it from the first moment he'd seen her. Maybe because she so looked like Olivia....

But he didn't need distractions, so he killed any further thought of her right there.

He picked up his clipboard with the notes he'd made so far—the list of necessary repairs to walls, ceiling, floors and windows was growing—and wandered aimlessly, eventually taking the stairs down to the only area of the wing that he hadn't yet searched.

The wine cellar had been abandoned last, after the giant casks that held the Slater vintage had been emptied. But they were still here, like hulking monoliths squatting under the beamed ceiling.

He walked among them, remembering he and Webb used to play hide-and-seek down here, wondering what secrets the casks might hold.

The place smelled moldy and he quickly found the source—a wall that looked as though it had been forever wet from the spring rains. Shining a flashlight on the beams and supports, Ross could see that the wood was rotting away. It was amazing the room hadn't collapsed in on itself before now. A testament, he guessed, to the way things used to be built—to last forever. With proper maintenance, Slater House would be forever.

When he'd bid for the job, he'd hoped to find something in the south wing. Some clue. Some piece of information that would shed some light on the past.

It was all nonsense, of course. What had he thought? That Webb would have left him a secret message in their old hiding place in the game room—which Ross had, of course, checked—and that he'd be able to use his kid-era decoder ring to solve the mystery?

Lost among the long-empty wine casks, Ross admitted the futility of trying to find the truth on his own, admitted his failure to himself. And recognized the growing sense of guilt he'd tried to ignore all these years.

He needed to make Frederick talk about the past and the old man wasn't going to do that easily.

Ross could only think of one thing that would give him the leverage he needed.

Melanie.

Chapter Seven

Working in documentary film had made Melanie an expert researcher. She had to know how to dig for information to do a credible job, so that was what she was going to do now—dig.

"Do you need help getting set up?" Andrew asked after showing her to a second-floor morning room with an Internet-accessible computer.

"Thanks for the offer, but it looks pretty straightforward."

A PC with all the bells and whistles, nineteen-inch LCD monitor, scanner and color printer, the state-of-the-art equipment was sharply at odds with the surrounding old-fashioned floral-print upholstery. A couch and two club chairs rounded the tile-faced fireplace, and the mahogany desk that Melanie was seated at was massive and hand-carved. It was set near a window that overlooked the walled garden below.

"I shall leave you to it, then."

"Uh-huh. Thanks, Andrew." She was already intent on the computer.

Just in case Andrew lingered a moment, Melanie brought up her e-mail as camouflage. She'd only been gone a day and already had thirty-something e-mails waiting for her. Nothing pressing. She breezed through them, deleting most, answering a few.

Then, after ascertaining she was alone, Melanie pulled up a search engine and began. It didn't take long for her to find dozens of references to something called genetic memory. Some neuroscientists believed DNA created memory molecules that stored information and passed it down to one's descendants.

Melanie read several of the articles, fascinated by what seemed to be the crux of the theory:

> *Many people experience such memories under hypnosis—the extreme of past life regression— whereas a more common event might be choosing to do something and not knowing why. It is probable that the choice is made based on past experiences of an ancestor without the person realizing what is happening.*

Such as her knowing about the library or the key or the game table, Melanie thought, or the vague recollection of having been in various rooms in the house.

She found many examples that reinforced the idea of genetic memory—as in the study of newborn calves that had never seen a cattle grid refusing to cross lines painted on a road to look like one.

One might call this instinct, but how is instinct passed from mother to child? Some scientists suggest that if instinct is passed through the DNA, then why not other forms of memory?

Was it possible? Could she somehow have inherited her mother's memories? They'd always had some kind of inexplicable connection—well, at least Melanie did. Her one-way street. Mother to daughter.

The theory was making sense.

And yet, why her? Why such blatant memories? Apparently some people—like her—simply had an added gift of some sort.

Melanie sat there for the longest time trying to digest what she'd read. Wondering if she could make the memories come to her, a thought that tightened her chest and lodged a lump in her throat.

Before leaving the computer, she had the presence of mind to erase its history and cache—her tracks. She didn't want the next person who sat down at the computer to know what she'd been researching. Not that it really mattered, she guessed. Most people wouldn't believe in genetic memory. She didn't know if she herself did quite yet.

But what else explained the memories?

Being here, in this house where her mother was raised, was triggering something. But only when she was alone, her mind working, searching…

She decided to search now.

Her mother must have spent time in this room.

Slowly, Melanie circled the perimeter, really looking at the details that her mother would have seen. As did every room in the house, it seemed, the morning room held a vase of fresh flowers. Pink and white roses.

Smiling, Melanie bent forward to take a whiff of their rich scent.

"What do you think you're doing, young lady?"

Melanie started and her heart began to pound. Knowing what was happening this time, she forced herself to relax, took another whiff of the roses and let herself drift....

"I'M ADMIRING the roses, Father," I say. "What is it you think I'm doing?"

"Playing the foolish young wench."

"Young wench?" I laugh and turn to face him. "This is 1981, not 1881."

"Do not mock me." He begins to pace in front of the fireplace. "I am concerned for you, Olivia."

"I've never given you cause—"

"Until now, perhaps not. But when you go against your class—"

"I'm not going against anything! And I don't believe in class structure. We're all created equal, remember?"

"Some of us being more equal than others."

"I won't define my friends by how much money they have."

"I'm not talking about friends. I've tolerated your friendship with that maid since you were a child. But your seeing a young man who is so inappropriate is out of the question."

I don't have to ask how he knows. I saw him speaking to John Grey earlier. John caught us together in the old wing. Still, I thought the private investigator was my friend. My mistake.

"Why can't you choose an escort more presentable? Why, Andrew Lennox—"

"Who I see is my business."

"Not while you're under my roof!"

I almost ask him if he wants me to leave, but I bite my tongue. He'll calm down, I tell myself.

He has to.

MELANIE BLINKED and her grandfather—a much younger version than she'd met—was gone.

So Mom hadn't gotten along with her father. No big surprise. He'd tried to control her into seeing a man he'd thought appropriate. Like Andrew. Which made her wonder about Andrew's take on the situation. Apparently he'd held her mother in high regard. Perhaps she could get information out of him.

Again Melanie wondered if her grandfather hadn't controlled her mother right out of the house.

Not that she believed it was that simple. Surely there had to be more to the story.

Besides, the memory had shown her that Mom hadn't been a weakling, that she'd stood up for herself.

What then?

These walls really could talk. If she kept at it, would they reveal what had happened all those years ago?

Melanie figured she'd have a lot of walls to visit

to get the whole story, when one person might be able to do the same in a single visit.

If she could find Janine Marsh.

Now was as good a time as any, Melanie decided, heading for her suite to freshen up.

If she was lucky, she might have her answers before the day was done.

VINCENT SLATER arrived home from his business trip with all the pomp of a reigning prince.

Which she guessed he was, Melanie thought, making her way down the stairs and watching his mother make over him as though he'd done something noteworthy just by showing up.

"Take his bags," Eleanor told one of the maids. "And you, let Father know Vincent is home." To a third young woman she said, "Tell Cook to whip up one of Vincent's favorites." The maids scurried off in different directions and Eleanor concentrated on her son. "I don't know how we get by a day without your being here."

"Probably by shopping," Vincent said drily.

"What a sense of humor!"

"I know." Vincent spoke to his mother but his dark gaze found Melanie's. "I could do a stand-up act."

"Seriously. You're home early. I didn't think you would be in until tonight."

"There is a matter I need to take care of."

Considering what she now knew—that Eleanor had lost her only other child—Melanie figured that gave her extra bragging rights for this one. Vincent had his mother's good looks and his father's dark hair and eyes. His suit was tailored and she was certain the watch he wore was a real Rolex. On her way out to Slater Corners—no introduction forthcoming as far as she could tell—Melanie continued on to the front door.

The phone rang and Eleanor said, "Drat, I'm expecting an important call about some musicians for Saturday. Don't you move," she commanded her son, waltzing off into the next room. "I want to hear about your trip."

Melanie reached the door just as Vincent said, "So you're my long-lost cousin—"

"Melanie," she said, turning to face him.

"Imagine how surprised we were to learn of your existence."

"Not as surprised as I was, believe me."

Vincent approached her, his gaze scanning her embroidered Bohemian handkerchief top and low-cut cropped pants without reflecting any judgments. "So your mother never talked about her family?"

Thinking at least one member of the family sounded interested in her, Melanie said, "Not a word."

"Yet you came running the moment you heard about Slater House."

Oops. Too soon to relax.

"Not the very moment," she clarified. "But after thinking about it, I felt it was important for me to meet the family I never knew."

In a way that he never could guess. He was older than she—mid to late thirties—so he'd been a half dozen years younger than Mom when she'd done her disappearing act.

Vincent asked, "So what do you think of the old place?"

"It's, um…well, huge."

"It is, isn't it?" He picked a piece of invisible lint off his lapel. "Just not big enough for us both."

Clenching her jaw at the broadside, Melanie stared at him a moment before saying, "So, how soon are *you* leaving?"

Vincent's smile tightened. "You do have a charming sense of humor."

Disappointed that her only cousin had turned out to be as suspicious of her as his mother, Melanie turned her back on him and left the house.

Normally she was a person who spoke her mind. Since she'd arrived it had taken great effort not to. Zinging Vincent in retaliation had been a mistake, she was certain. Too impulsive. She should have tried to allay his suspicion rather than feed it. No doubt he would be watching her even more closely now. Forget his telling her anything of value.

Hoping for better luck with a nonfamily member, away from this house that was having a negative effect on her, she was determined to find Janine Marsh.

Before leaving the property, she swung by the south wing. No red Jaguar. No Ross….

Why was she even looking for him?

The kiss. That was it. So unexpected. So…

Ross Bennet could be aggravating, she remembered as she passed the blind curve, but he could also be charming and, yes, seductive.

In another time, another place…

But it wasn't. And she wasn't here to hook up with anyone. She had to focus, focus, focus. Even with determination, it took her the length of the ride into town to put out of mind the impression Ross had made on her.

Slater Corners was a reflection of the great estate that had spawned it. Several blocks of shops and restaurants and small businesses were housed in connected stone and brick buildings that looked as if they'd been designed by the same architect who'd been responsible for Slater House.

Melanie drove around, looking for women's boutiques. There were several, in fact. Not knowing where to start, she simply picked one—Forever Young—and pulled her car into the lot behind it.

The store was upscale, the prices matching any place on North Michigan Avenue.

Melanie pretended interest in some shawls that started at two hundred dollars and went up while waiting for a saleswoman to come by. There were three that she could see. One appeared to be in her late twenties or early thirties, one in her sixties. The third woman might be her mother's age. It was the twentysomething who finally strolled over to her, saying, "Can I help you find what you want?"

"I hope so. Does this come in other colors?" she asked, holding up a turquoise shawl embroidered with a beaded peacock.

"I believe we have that in cream, also." The saleswoman dug around in a drawer beneath the display. "Ah, here it is."

Though she'd been hoping the woman wouldn't find it—two hundred dollars was stretching her budget a bit—Melanie said, "Great, I'll take it." Hopefully a sale would make the woman open up.

The woman rang up her credit card and packaged the shawl in a box.

Melanie waited until she was putting the box into a shopping bag before asking, "Do you know Janine Marsh?"

"Janine Marsh? Mmm, can't say that she's been in here."

"Actually, I was told she worked at one of the local boutiques. Maybe she married, so the last name's different. Anyone named Janine? Or Jannie?"

The saleswoman frowned. "I'm afraid not."

"Thanks anyway."

Melanie left the package in the trunk of her car before setting off for the next shop. No luck there, either. Nor at the third shop she checked. But she didn't leave any of the shops empty-handed.

Only a few more clothing boutiques. Melanie began to wonder if she was limiting herself. The term women's boutique could include things other than clothing. Shoes. Gifts. If she had to, she would visit every shop in town.

Intent on her plan, Melanie almost ran into a man rounding the corner.

Ross.

The first thing that came to mind was that kiss they'd shared. The second thing was that she needed a clear head if she was going to get the answers she needed. And she definitely didn't have a clear head when she was around Ross.

Not the way he was staring at her so intently that her heart began drumming in response.

"So," he said, "you fled the estate to take a break from the family."

"Maybe I thought I was finally going someplace where I wouldn't run into you."

Ross laughed. "That's a switch…considering you've been chasing me since you arrived."

"Don't get a swelled head—or anything else—just because I needed someone to talk to this morning."

"I noticed you found someone willing to listen."

"Andrew?" She shrugged. "Nice man. He brought me up to speed about the fate of Slater grandchildren. No wonder everyone is so sour."

"The Slaters have always been a reckless bunch. You included."

"Sad for Helen, especially, losing both her children and then her husband."

"You would have liked Nicholas. He was the best of the bunch. Along with Olivia, of course."

The mention of her mother gave Melanie a case of the guilts. She hated lying. Not that this was *her* lie.

"It would have been nice to have someone in my camp." Someone she really could talk to, Melanie thought.

"I was just stopping by my office to sign some

letters that have to go out. If you care to drop by, you can have a look at the blueprints of the south wing."

Why the switch? she wondered. Ross knew how to keep her on edge, alternating between sarcasm and seduction. Considering he'd caught her exploring the south wing twice, he had to know she couldn't resist.

"Intriguing invitation," she murmured.

Thinking she could continue her search for the former maid the next day, Melanie wasn't sure if she was going for a look at the blueprints or to spend more time with the man. She had to admit he was attractive, that when she was around him her pulse beat faster. He challenged her, stimulated her, made her look forward to their next encounter.

Maybe it had to do with his age. He had a certain sophistication she wasn't used to in the young creative types she usually dated. He seemed more sure of himself. Something positive to say about maturity.

Ross's office was on the next block, located on a corner, the shingle over the door reading Bennet Restorations. His assistant, Claire—a stylish brunette who looked to be thirty—was on the telephone when they entered. Ross waved to her and kept on straight into his office.

The organized mess made Melanie feel right at home. Ross's work style wasn't so different from hers. Rather than movie posters on the walls, however, he had framed photos of old homes and other buildings.

"You have a degree as an architect, right? So with all the new development going on in the area, what made you choose restoration?"

"Living on the estate gave me an appreciation of history. I guess I never got over it."

"But are there enough old houses in the area to keep you busy?"

"My company consists of me and Claire and an intern who works part-time. I draw up the plans and oversee the restoration, but the actual work, both interior design and labor, is subcontracted. That means I'm not confined to this area. And I don't only do houses. I just finished restoring an old market in Charlotte into tourist shops. And before that, I had the pleasure of turning an old movie palace in Lexington into a theater for concerts and touring musicals."

Even as he talked about his work, she could see it coming to life in her mind's eye. "Following you through a project would make a great documentary."

"Not that films about restorations haven't been done before. You'd have to find some sort of spin to make it unique."

Exactly what she'd been thinking. Melanie couldn't believe how in tune they were.

"Maybe you're the linchpin," she said, getting excited now. "At least in the case of Slater House. 'Son of worker brings house back to former glory' and all that."

No sooner were the words out of Melanie's mouth than she regretted them. Ross's features stiffened and there was a coldness in his gaze. It only lasted a minute and then was gone so quickly she might have imagined it.

Only she hadn't.

"I need to get to those papers," he said, the warmth in his tone gone. "The blueprints are over there." He waved a hand toward the desk. "Have a look."

Melanie turned her attention away from Ross to the abandoned wing. Just as she'd surmised, the ballroom and foyer took up two-thirds of the first floor. And there was the game room, where Ross had kissed her.

Thinking about it again shot warmth through Melanie.

He interested her, and not only as the person who would restore the abandoned wing.

She concentrated harder on the blueprints. The second and third floors seemed similar to the main house in that each floor had several suites of rooms with baths, plus large individual rooms that seemed to be sitting parlors. Below the first floor was what looked to be a wine cellar. Of course, that made sense since one of the family businesses was a vineyard.

Taking in the details, Melanie noted two staircases—one in the ballroom, a second at the far end of the foyer. But it looked as if there was a third, also in the ballroom. She was running fingertips along that staircase, wondering how she'd missed it, when she realized Ross was standing behind her, so she could imagine the feel of his body against hers....

"Something interesting?"

"This staircase—I was trying to place it."

"It's behind the walls. The servants used it to get from one floor to the other."

"Was that common?"

"In a house this size," he said, his breath ruffling the back of her hair.

She couldn't move. Rather, she was afraid to move. He was so close behind her she could feel his heat. It slid along her nerves, tried to steal her breath.

"So what do you think?"

She thought she ought to get out of here. "Impressive. Especially the wine cellar. I can't believe that was abandoned, too."

"It happened before your grandfather's time. Probably sometime after Prohibition was repealed."

Turning carefully, she brushed against him. The light contact was enough to elicit a reaction from her—warmth pooled low in her stomach and her nipples tightened.

Praying he didn't notice, Melanie asked, "Are you saying my great-great-grandfather ran a speakeasy?"

"Probably only for his friends. I know a lot about the house's history. If you'd like to hear it I'd be happy to share…say, over dinner?"

"Dinner," she agreed, thinking there was another history she wanted to talk about. Her mother's. "I'd probably better call the house and let them know not to set a place for me."

OLIVIA ENTERED THE HOUSE exhausted but feeling triumphant after closing a big deal.

Still, a subtle but constant worry niggled at her, and nothing she did would shake it.

She would feel better if John Grey had never

found her or Melanie. She hadn't been able to put out of mind Melanie's hurt and anger at the necessary lies. Even if her daughter's message earlier had made it sound like nothing had happened, Olivia knew Melanie was good at covering her feelings. Thankfully, she hadn't been tempted to accept her grandfather's invitation to visit Slater House.

Olivia finally had a chance to return Melanie's call. She'd been tied up with business all day and hadn't felt comfortable getting into a personal conversation with a new client in tow. Melanie's voice mail answered.

"Hey, sweetheart, just returning your call." Disappointed that she missed her daughter, she said, "I had a big day, a big sale." Usually she and Melanie would celebrate together. She had to keep in mind her daughter had her own life now. "I'm bushed, so I'll talk to you tomorrow."

Though she made a quick bite to eat, she wasn't really hungry and so found herself wandering around the house, tired but too wired to sleep. She might as well do something productive, she thought, sorting the mail into piles—bills, trash, miscellaneous. She was about to sit down when she realized the red eye of the answering machine was blinking at her.

When she hit play and heard John Grey's voice— he asked her to call him—her knees grew weak. She held on to the credenza as she listened to the second message, also from him.

"I was hoping you'd return my call," he rasped. "I hate leaving this on your machine but I guess I don't got a choice. Melanie is here, Olivia. I swear it's not my doing. I never heard from her after you came to see me. She arrived this morning. I just thought you'd want to know."

Olivia gasped, remembering Melanie's promise to her.

But Melanie hadn't actually promised that she wouldn't go to North Carolina. She'd merely promised she wouldn't call John Grey.

Olivia tried not to panic. Surely her daughter would be in no immediate danger.

But how could she be certain?

The longer Melanie was there, the more imminent the threat. Knowing Father, he would find myriad ways to keep his newly found granddaughter from leaving, and the longer Melanie was there, the less likely it would be that she would leave unscathed.

Olivia picked up the phone, but she didn't want to leave a cryptic message for her daughter.

It took but the space of a heartbeat for her to know what she had to do. Adrenaline shot through her as she replaced the phone in its cradle. She couldn't warn Melanie. She simply had to rescue her foolish daughter.

Quickly packing an overnight bag and leaving a note for the cleaning lady that she was going out of town, she left the house. It was late, too late to get a plane. But she could drive and be in North Carolina by noon. She couldn't just sit around and do nothing. She had to act now or she would go out of her mind with worry.

It was only when she was in her car and on the road

that Olivia thought to call John to let *him* know she'd gotten his messages and was on her way. His voice mail answered. Unfortunately her cell ran out of juice before she could decide whether or not to leave a message.

"Damn!"

Realizing she'd left the charger at home, Olivia thought to pick up a spare battery, but realistically that wouldn't happen until she hit Asheville. She considered finding a pay phone to call Melanie, to tell her daughter to get out of that house now!

That might be a mistake. A warning. Melanie wouldn't sit on a command like that. She would cause a stir, not knowing where that could lead.

But Olivia knew.

In the quiet of the night, she examined the enormity of her decision. This wasn't simply a matter of pulling Melanie out of harm's way. John's finding her and her daughter had been a sign, one she'd chosen to ignore.

She couldn't ignore what had happened any longer.

Tears welled in her eyes and spilled over her cheeks. The past had caught up to her at last. She had to face it. Deal with it. Make things right.

She was wondering how the hell she could manage that without Melanie finding out the whole ugly truth, when the car began to shake, followed by a loud sound like a gunshot.

Chapter Eight

Ross knew the old man wasn't going to like his wining and dining one of the Slater heirs, but he really didn't care. He had an ironclad contract on the restoration deal, so Frederick couldn't oust *him* from the estate.

It gave him an odd sense of power to know that he could see Melanie without consequences. If he didn't already have an incentive for wanting to spend time with her, that alone would do it for him.

"This way," Ross said.

He placed a hand at the small of her back to guide her to the Jag and felt a shudder go through her.

Stiffening slightly, she said, "I'm capable of getting wherever on my own."

He removed the hand. "Turn right here." Then he murmured, "Don't worry, I'm not going to kiss you again."

She gave him a look that would freeze a lesser man. "You caught me off guard before."

"I caught you? You're the one who asked to be kissed."

Ross realized two elderly ladies were standing in a store doorway glued to their conversation.

"Just broadcast it, why don't you?" Melanie mumbled, shouldering past him to race down the street.

Ross lengthened his stride to keep up with her. Melanie was so different from most of the women he knew—genteel Southern women who would never give him grief in the open way this one did. She had spirit and seemed fearless. Thinking about the best way to make a connection with her, he thought about her enthusiasm for her work. And for his. Remembering their conversation about Slater House history, he knew he could continue to interest her as he restored the old wing.

He had to admit Melanie wasn't hard to look at. She would be a bright spot wherever she went. Literally. He openly checked out her colorful Bohemian outfit. The see-through blouse alone would send Frederick around the bend.

The thought of using her to get to the old man gave him a twinge of regret, but he had to keep in mind his ultimate goal. If this was the only way, then he had no choice.

Once at the Jaguar, he helped her into the passenger seat, then jumped over the closed door to get behind the wheel.

"Isn't that a little reckless?" she asked.

"It's one of the main reasons to own a convertible."

He pulled out onto the main road through town and headed away from everything Slater.

"Where are we headed?" she asked.

"I thought you might like a look at Asheville."

"Sounds good."

In reality Ross figured it was less likely that they'd be interrupted by someone who knew him. Or her. The Slaters might show up anywhere around here.

Despite his intent, Ross wanted to know Melanie on a whole other level, one that would admittedly send Frederick ballistic. That kiss had left him with an itch he couldn't get out of his mind. Getting physically entangled with Melanie would complicate things, however, so he would play it cool and keep things between them strictly on a friendly level.

All he needed was to develop enough of a relationship with her to have leverage with Frederick. It would take something major to make the old man open up to him about the past that he'd hidden for so long.

Unless he was mistaken, Melanie was major.

"So how did you get into restoration architecture?" she asked.

"I worked for a large firm for several years. I'd just finished some grad studies in architectural preservation and American architectural history when we got the contract to do one of the old government buildings in D.C. I was the junior member of the team that prepared research reports and worked on the plans and specifications for the project."

"What made you decide to go it alone?"

"I was a small cog in a big company. I wanted to be in charge of restoration projects, and it didn't look like that was going to happen anytime soon. So at the first opportunity, I made my move."

The drive into the city was fast—barely fifteen minutes—and since it was still early, there wasn't any wait at the bistro Ross chose. They sat outside—it was one of several restaurants grouped together with an outdoor eating area—and ordered a couple of house specials and sweet tea.

"I'm going to be addicted to this stuff," Melanie said as she lifted the tall glass and sipped.

Ross watched, fascinated, as her throat surged with her long swallow. "It can be addictive," he murmured, not meaning the tea itself.

"What's in this?"

"Other than black tea? A cup or two of sugar to the gallon, depending on who makes it."

"Yikes."

"No sweet tea at home, I take it?"

"In Chicago?" She shook her head. "This place is different in lots of ways."

"Is that good or bad?"

She shrugged. "No judgments."

All the while they'd been talking, she kept her gaze roaming, as if she were trying to absorb every detail of the area. The history of the buildings, but more than that, the citizenry…artsy twentysome-things…the family of five with three stepping-stone little kids…the elderly lady walking her bichon frise.

"You're really interested in people, aren't you?"

"Everyone has a story."

"And you like telling them."

"Some more than others."

Remembering her comment at dinner the night

before, he saw an opportunity to get her to open up. "You must be anxious to get back to work."

"I'm just wrapping up my latest documentary," she said. "I need to do my editing notes while the interviews are still fresh in my mind. There's a certain momentum to a film and when that gets interrupted…"

"Even for a few days?"

"It's already been a few days. My grandfather is making it difficult for me to leave with that party he's holding in my honor."

"Frederick does like the world to spin his way."

She twisted a piece of bread with her fingers— long, nicely tapered, heavy with rings and tipped with short nails the same magenta as the narrow streaks in her hair.

"You don't sound like you approve," she said.

"If it has to do with *things*—like work—that's fine. But when it comes to people, he can be a real bastard."

His honesty drove Melanie to silence for a moment. Did she think he was being unfair? She wouldn't for long. Unless Frederick Slater had mellowed—which Ross doubted—Melanie would have a bigger dose of the old man in the next several days than would make her comfortable.

"You know, forget what I said. Try to enjoy your forced vacation at Slater House."

Melanie laughed. "Just navigating through the maze of rooms is work. Do you know how much time it takes just to get to breakfast, for example? At home, I roll out of bed and a few steps later I'm in my kitchen."

"Where *you* have to do the cooking."

"I don't mind. I like taking care of myself. Mom taught me to be self-sufficient from the time I was a little kid. I liked it. Made me feel grown-up like her." Melanie gave him a considering look. "I can't help wondering, though, that she was so happy. I mean, she was raised in luxury with servants to grant her every wish. How could she give it all up?"

"Maybe being happy is the clue," Ross said tactfully. "Making her own way allowed her to find a happiness she couldn't find in her father's home. So perhaps she wasn't any more suited to servants and a mansion than you claim to be."

Melanie shook her head. "No, that's not it. I mean, yes, you might have a point, but she never looked back, left her family behind for good. Something must have gone terribly wrong. You knew her. Any clues as to what might have happened to make her chuck her life and start a new one?"

Ross could hardly believe it. She was turning the tables on him, trying to get *him* to talk. She was good at this. Must be her experience drilling her documentary subjects.

"Your grandfather is a controlling man."

"But my mother is a strong woman."

Remembering the situation, Ross said, "Maybe back then she wasn't strong enough."

"I think she was."

"Before your time. How do you know she didn't get all that strength by being responsible for you?"

Melanie stared at him for a moment. He sensed

she wanted to say something. At the same time, she seemed reluctant.

"What?" he asked. "Out with it."

She took a big breath and said, "Mom refused to let her father choose her escorts."

"Olivia told you that?"

Melanie lapsed into silence for a moment and Ross felt the space between them grow electric.

What did she know?

He tightened his hand around his glass and waited her out.

Finally she asked, "Do you believe in psychic connections and all that implies?"

"You mean, like knowing when something is going to happen? Sure. I think some people are sensitive."

"What about all of a sudden knowing stuff that *did* happen? In the past? To someone else?"

"I don't get your point."

"Ever since I arrived at Slater House, I've known things that I had no reason to know," Melanie said. "Such as where the door to the library was or that there was a chess table in that game room."

"You don't have to be psychic to have intuition."

"There's more. Several weird things have happened to me…I got on the Internet and did some research. Ever heard of genetic memory?"

"As in having memories passed down through your genes?"

"More specifically, through DNA."

"*Twilight Zone* stuff."

"Not so much. Melanie Pierce stuff."

Seeming uncomfortable at the admission, Melanie shifted in her seat. Even so, she kept her gaze locked with his, giving Ross a weird feeling. She was serious.

"Are you saying you're having someone else's memories?" he asked, trying not to sound too disbelieving. "Olivia's?"

She nodded. "They're Mom's, all right." Her breathing quickened as she said, "It's like I'm suddenly in a movie and I *become* her."

Well, that was more than a bit much to swallow. "Or your imagination is working overtime."

"Is that why I had an entire conversation with Jannie?"

He stared at her for a moment then said, "Your mother must have told you about Jannie."

"No."

"They were best friends."

"Mom never mentioned her. Well, at least not that I remember."

"Okay, that's odd, but she could have mentioned Jannie when you were really little and being at Slater House dragged the memory—*your* memory—out of you."

"But not the fact that they were talking about a boy. An inappropriate boy Mom was set on seeing."

Ross stiffened, but told himself it could merely be a good guess. He waited for her to explain and so was disappointed when she turned the direction.

"You don't by any chance know where I can find Jannie, do you?"

"Sorry. Not a clue. I see her around sometimes, but it's just in passing."

Obviously disappointed, Melanie frowned. "Then there's the chess table in the game room," she went on. "My grandfather used to play with the Gray & Blue set. He was always Gray. And I—I mean Mom—the guy taught her to play at that table…well, at least I think so. You interrupted before I could see what happened."

The kiss, Ross thought. He'd known Melanie hadn't quite been all there, but he never could have guessed… A little unnerved, he realized this was hitting way too close to home.

Deciding he was playing into her fantasy, he gave himself a mental shake. There had to be a logical explanation for everything she was telling him. Olivia could have told her all this and she was lying. But why would Melanie do that? It didn't make sense. None of this did.

He said, "The whole chess thing is something else your mother might have mentioned."

"No. She told me my grandfather—not to mention anyone else she was connected to, including my father—was dead."

"So you never knew your father."

Melanie shrugged. "He died before I was born."

Which gave Ross pause. He'd assumed… "What about your father's family?"

"Mom told me he never told her where to find them. That he simply said they were estranged and she didn't want to push it. I thought they might be dead, too. But now it seems to me the story was part of her cover…."

Frowning, she downed her sweet tea and lapsed into silence. Ross knew she was wondering about her father. He wanted to know more about the weird memory thing.

"So what are you saying? How exactly are you getting these memories?"

"It only happens when I'm alone." Her gaze was clear, free of artifice when she said, "I hear a voice and the next thing I know I'm thrown backward in time. Always to the same time—right before Mom left Slater House."

As if the house itself were trying to tell Melanie something, Ross mused. Before he could follow up on that line of thought, the waitress arrived with their food—tilapia with mango salsa and sweet potato fries.

Melanie dug in with enthusiasm—or perhaps she was simply glad to escape the path the topic had taken.

Pursuing it would get him nothing more—she couldn't tell him what she didn't know. It was enough, however, to satisfy one question he'd carried with him all these years.

Something bad had happened at Slater House. Talk about intuition. Ross had known something was wrong all along. If only they hadn't been ousted from the property, he could have investigated the abandoned wing years ago….

He had his chance now, not that he'd found anything yet. Too late? Or was he searching in all the wrong places? Looking at Melanie, he wondered if there was something to memories being passed along through DNA, after all.

And if there was a way he could get her to retrieve Olivia's memories and solve the mystery of that last night the Bennets had lived on Slater land.

MELANIE FELT HERSELF tense up as Ross slowed his car next to hers. They were back in Slater Corners after a nice evening—dinner, a tour of Asheville, dessert at a European pastry shop—and she hoped he wouldn't spoil it now.

He said, "I really should follow you home."

"No need." She couldn't help the tightness in her voice.

"Danger junkie alert."

Irritated, she said, "I really don't need anyone's protection. And I really need to go." She opened the passenger door. "Thanks for everything."

But before she could get out, Ross was out of the car, extending his hand. She took it and he steadied her as she got to her feet.

"Afraid Frederick will see us together?"

She didn't miss the censure in his tone. He was correct, of course. She didn't want to stir up her grandfather's ire by letting him in on the identity of her dinner companion. As far as her relatives were concerned, she'd gotten carried away shopping and had treated herself to an evening away from the family chaos.

"I'm my own person. I can see whomever I want. My grandfather isn't going to start dictating my movements."

"He's managed to stop you from going back to Chicago when you want."

"That's different." Considering how little she'd learned about the past in two whole days, she wasn't ready to go anyway.

"Different how?"

"No biggie. He wants me to meet his friends."

"You really think that's all there is to it? Then let me be your escort."

Her heart thumped at the suggestion, but whether from excitement or dread, she wasn't certain. Bringing Ross to a party with a hundred of her grandfather's closest friends and associates… The vision of her grandfather and mother arguing came back to her. Instinctively she doubted he would consider Ross suitable suitor material, successful restoration architect or not.

So she hedged. "I've already been asked."

"You let your grandfather choose your escort?"

"No. Andrew asked me on his own."

"Andrew."

"There's nothing wrong with Andrew."

"Other than a huge age difference. But I guess you might find him safe." When she didn't bite, Ross said, "So you're really going with him."

"I told him I would think about it."

His forehead furrowed into a frown and she could almost physically feel his disapproval.

"While you're thinking," he said, his voice low, sending a thrill through her, "think about this."

Ross slipped a hand behind her neck and angled

her head so he could more easily kiss her. Melanie knew she should stop him immediately, but her flesh was telling her otherwise. Pinned against the car, it responded to his heat with a need that couldn't be met in public.

Even so, she didn't push him away as instinct bade her do. She kissed him back...wrapped her arms around his neck...made a gasping sound when his hand found the side of her breast. His thumb flicked over the nipple and her response was to push harder against his hand.

Suddenly, Ross pulled her so close and tight that she felt his erection through their clothes. He slipped his mouth to her ear, the heat of his breath there along with the heat of him against her setting her on fire inside.

Oh, how she wanted him to go further. He was no boy like her usual dates. He would know what to do with a woman to make her wildest sexual fantasies come true.

Then suddenly Ross let her go and even in the dim parking lot light she could see his satisfaction reflected in his expression.

"That's just a taste of what we could have together. So do think about it," he said. "About my taking you to the party."

Melanie gaped at him and was trying to find words to the effect *not if you were the last man on earth* when he left her and got back behind the wheel of the Jaguar.

Furious, she threw herself into the rental and

slammed the door. Hard. Even as she started her engine, she swore she heard his laughter.

She drove off, refusing to look back until she was on the forest road home.

How dare he try to manipulate her! As if she would let him. He'd had the nerve to criticize her grandfather for the very same trait. Did he really want to see her or was he simply trying to prove something to her? And to himself. She'd known letting down her guard with him would be dangerous, but she'd done it all the same.

Not again, she promised herself. From now on, she would be on guard.

Ross Bennet could be a dream come true…or her worst nightmare.

She would be crazy if she chose to find out which.

Chapter Nine

As she entered the house, Melanie heard a commotion. Raised voices. An exclamation of horror from one of the women.

Seeing her uncle Martin exiting the parlor as if he were relieved to be free of it, she couldn't help asking, "What's going on?"

"It's the private investigator who found you. John Grey."

"He's making all that ruckus?"

"The ruckus is over *him*. He's dead. Murdered."

Grey dead? Melanie went cold inside. "How? When?"

"Head bashed in," her uncle said matter-of-factly, sounding as if that weren't an unusual and horrible thing. "Apparently happened sometime last night. His girl found him sprawled in his office this afternoon. Seems she'd been working in the next room all morning, didn't even know he was there until she went to find a file."

Melanie swayed and tasted bile at the back of her throat. "My Lord…someone I know murdered."

Her mind immediately went into paranoid mode. Why was Grey killed?

Did it have something to do with *her?*

"The authorities have already been here, of course, questioning Father."

"Why?" Surely they didn't think her grandfather had committed murder.

"Grey has done work for Father for years. He was on permanent retainer."

Her grandfather had needed a P.I. at his beck and call? Mostly for business reasons, no doubt.

Martin went on. "It's only natural the detective in charge thought Father might know something of any problems Grey was having with a certain shady client."

"So they have a lead?"

"They found Sam Hale's file half hidden not far from the body. He's a local, an ex-con with violent tendencies."

"A file near the body." Melanie considered that for a moment. Yes, most criminals weren't the brightest bulbs, but this careless? "Doesn't that seem…well, awfully convenient?"

Martin's face grew red all the way into his receding hairline, his blue eyes bugged out and he began sputtering. "A-are you q-questioning the authorities?"

He sounded as if he was insulted she was questioning *him.* "Well, I—"

"They know what they're doing and if they say

Sam Hale is the chief suspect, it's not up to you to say differently."

With that, he stormed off, leaving Melanie gaping after him.

John Grey dead, the victim of foul play. She couldn't fathom it. Furthermore, she feared the worst—that his finding *her* had been the reason for his murder.

She had to talk to her mother, to find out what Mom knew. To warn her. How without admitting that she was in North Carolina? She had to, that was all there was to it. Mom would go nuts. Damn!

Slipping back outside, she plunked down on a bench and let the cool night breeze play over her for a moment. A faint scent of azaleas washed over her, both sweet and spicy like cloves. Calmer now, she turned on her cell and saw that she had a message.

Yep, she'd missed her mom's call. Her mother was going to bed early and said she'd talk to her tomorrow.

Not wanting to go inside just yet, Melanie made a couple of business calls, let her camera operator and editor know that she would be gone longer than she'd expected.

Thinking about her mother, she told herself that she'd gotten a short reprieve—that maybe she'd overreacted. Melanie hoped that Grey had, indeed, been killed by a dangerous client. Nothing to do with her.

She retrieved her purchases from the trunk of the car and went inside. The house was quiet now. Apparently her relatives had all retired to their quarters.

In the midst of watering plants in the garden room, the butler said, "Good evening, miss."

"So am I in trouble for skipping out on dinner?"

"Mr. Frederick has been happier."

"Is he given to waiting up for errant grandchildren?"

"Not to my knowledge. But I'm sure you will hear from him come morning."

Melanie sighed.

"Sorry, miss. Is there anything I can get you?"

"As in food? No, I'm well fed."

"Anything else?" He indicated her packages. "I can carry those for you."

Melanie laughed. "I'm perfectly capable of handling my own purchases. But I could use a little information…." She had to be crazy to be doing this. "About Ross Bennet."

"Ah," he said, his tone saying now he understood.

"He lived here as a boy, right?"

Johnson nodded. "His father was the stable master, his grandfather the head groundskeeper."

"Ross doesn't seem to like *my* grandfather much. And yet he's chosen to work for him, also. Whatever went wrong?"

"It's not my place to say, miss."

So he was being the loyal servant. "No speculation or judgments," Melanie said. "Just the facts. Please. What does Ross have against my grandfather? I need to know so that I can be prepared."

Her argument obviously swayed the reluctant butler. "I suppose it wouldn't hurt to share the bare facts. You could get those from anyone who knew the Bennets."

"Yes, of course," she said, her understanding expression meant to encourage him to continue.

"After the family was asked to leave the estate," Johnson went on, "Ross's father began drinking heavily. Eventually Thomas died of alcohol poisoning. His grandfather Benjamin is alive, but I'm told the old man lives with a broken heart still. Benjamin was born on the estate as were his father and grandfather before him. He was near retirement when the family was uprooted."

Uprooted…a nice way of saying they'd been kicked off the property. A father who'd drunk himself to death…a grandfather who still mourned the loss of his lifetime home…things that would be difficult for Ross to forgive, and certainly impossible to forget, Melanie thought.

That explained a lot of things, maybe even his strange behavior with her. Perhaps he didn't trust her—her being a Slater and all—and wanted the upper hand to protect himself. Given the circumstances, she could hardly blame him.

At least not for that.

But was he using her to make some kind of point to her grandfather? Possible. Probable? Melanie would like to think Ross was truly attracted to her as she was to him, but there was simply too much history here for her to be naive.

Before she could ask Johnson *why* the Bennets had been tossed off the estate, a low buzz caught the butler's attention. He reached into his pocket and checked the pager.

"That would be Mr. Frederick."

"Don't keep him waiting. I'm certain he's not in the best of moods as it is."

The butler crossed to a small caged elevator to one side of the garden room and rode up to her grandfather's quarters on the third floor.

Melanie took the stairs up to her room, all the while thinking about how her evening with Ross had ended. It really had been all good up until after the kiss.

She was still angry…and still interested, danger junkie that she was.

Maybe talking to Johnson about him had been a mistake, though. He was loyal to her grandfather. She could only hope he would be discreet.

Once in her room, she tossed the bags on a chair. She was too wired and it was too early to sleep, so she would continue her investigation of the house. If she were lucky, she might find the next piece of the puzzle.

Not wanting to poke around the abandoned wing at night, Melanie decided to stay in the main house. There were dozens of rooms she hadn't yet seen, just on the first floor. It was late—after ten—and she figured this would be a good time to explore without interruption. If someone did cross her path and asked what she was doing, she would merely say that since she was used to retiring at a later hour, she was simply taking the time to get the lay of the land. Which she would be doing if in a more complicated manner.

Too bad she had to be alone to connect with the past. Part of her—the danger-loving part—wanted Ross with her, witness to whatever did happen.

She could do better than that, she thought, digging the camcorder out of her bag and attaching the strap that would allow her to hang it off her shoulder. She could explore the house and record hands-free.

Waiting until she got downstairs, which seemed truly deserted, Melanie turned on the camera and set it to record. Then she headed in the direction of the stables. She hadn't been in any of these rooms before.

The music room came first. Though her mother had never played an instrument to her knowledge, she wandered past the piano and tried to lose herself as she had in the upstairs parlor. Nothing. She continued the circuit past a music stand and chair and a cabinet holding various smaller instruments. Not a whisper.

Apparently, Mom had never been a musical person.

Disappointed, she moved on, this time perusing a sitting room with embroidery stretched on a frame. Unable to imagine Eleanor doing anything that took such patience, she concluded the embroidery must belong to Helen. Touching the cloth, she closed her eyes to let her mind float. No connect.

Melanie sighed.

Surely her mother had been in every room in the house. So why did some speak to her and others not?

The next room was the mudroom with a door that led outside. Glancing out across the courtyard, she looked straight at the stables, when she had that feeling…

"I don't like this sneaking around."

The words were whispered directly into her ear,

sending a shiver of gooseflesh down her spine. Melanie let herself go, felt arms around her, a body pressed against hers.

"I DON'T LIKE IT, either, but I don't know what Father would do if he found out." I push against his chest so I can have some breathing room. "He wants me to see someone more…appropriate."

"Like Andrew Lennox. You're not really letting that guy escort you to the party?"

"Just to make Father happy. It doesn't mean anything, I promise."

I look into his green eyes and my knees grow weak. I want more than anything to go to the party with him. But I can't start another argument with Father over it. Sometimes I'm not quite as brave as I would like to be.

"I don't like it, Olivia."

Neither did I, but rationalized that I was buying time. "I'll be thinking of you the whole night."

But he isn't so easily appeased. His expression is dark, his jaw stubbornly set.

"I'm going to be an architect," he says. "I've already been accepted into the program. Someday, I'll have my own business. What more does he want?"

"The proper breeding. He would probably like you to have papers just as he has for his Thoroughbreds."

A HORSE'S WHINNY snapped Melanie back to the present, leaving her breathless.

Mom's boyfriend…the dark hair, thick-lashed green eyes, rugged cheekbones…so familiar…

Could she really have seen a much younger Ross?

Freaked by the possibility that her mother and Ross had been a couple, that he'd been responsible for driving Mom from her home somehow, she abandoned her exploration for the night and hurried back to her quarters.

Melanie didn't stop until she entered her bedroom, where she threw herself on the bed.

How had she done this? Opened herself to the very person who might hold the key to her mother's flight from Slater House? Why hadn't Ross said anything—maybe not at first, but tonight, when she'd shared the genetic memory theory?

She should have known better than to trust him, Melanie thought, unprepared for the emotions warring through her. She *had* known, but it hadn't seemed to matter.

What was wrong with her? She hardly knew the man. So why did she feel so disappointed?

Deciding to check the video, she found the footage in the mudroom and, using a headset, played it back.

Of course, the room was deserted and the only sounds she heard were those of her own voice.

I don't like it, either, but I don't know what Father would do if he found out.

Was that why Ross's family had been tossed off the estate? Because of his involvement with her mother?

She'd wondered why Ross had agreed to work for her grandfather. Now she was amazed that her grandfather would do business with Ross.

And what did he want with *her?* Was he attracted to her or to her money? Or did his motive have something to do with getting even with her grandfather as she'd guessed before?

If she were smart, she would stay away from the man.

Only…she couldn't….

Unless she was totally imagining these visions, Ross was her best bet at finding out what really had happened to make Mom run. She would do whatever it took—even some manipulation of her own—to see that nothing more happened to her mother.

Chapter Ten

Melanie got a pass on the confrontation she thought would happen over breakfast. Her grandfather wasn't there. No one was. Relieved, she ate alone and relaxed a little. Not that it lasted long. The butler caught her before she could return to her room where she would clean up and then hit Slater Corners to again look for Jannie.

"Mr. Frederick would like to see you in his study at precisely nine o'clock, miss."

"How worried should I be?"

Again the proper servant, Johnson said, "I'm afraid I wouldn't know."

Her morning ruined—she would rather have had it out than wait for an unpleasant encounter—Melanie went back to her quarters, where she tried again to call her mother.

Again she got the answering machine and voice mail. She left two messages—a bit more insistent this time.

Frustrated, she lay back on her bed and tried to

meditate, but every time she closed her eyes, she saw the dark-haired young man in her memory.

If that hadn't been a young Ross, she didn't know who it could be.

If only she could contact her mother, she would ask her. Enough of the secrets. How was she supposed to protect her mother when she didn't know the nature of the danger?

Not wanting to dwell on the questions she couldn't answer at the moment, Melanie decided to head back downstairs even though she was a bit early. No doubt her grandfather would be waiting for her, ready to lecture her on the importance of the family name or some such. She might as well deal with him and be done with it.

Opposite the library and overlooking the gardens, the study wasn't any more modest than the other rooms in the house. The lower walls were of oak wainscoting; the upper portion looked to be covered with real leather in a deep red. A half dozen matching leather chairs were set in a semicircle around a massive—and currently unoccupied—carved mahogany desk.

Helen sat in one of the chairs. Having thought she alone was about to face her grandfather, Melanie realized she'd been wrong. She'd been wanting to talk to Helen in private, so she sat next to her.

"What's going on?" Melanie asked.

"I wouldn't know." Helen's voice was cool. She was staring at her hands in her lap.

"I'm really sorry about hurting your feelings, Helen. I didn't know about Louisa." Melanie reached out and covered the woman's hands with her own. "My sincere condolences."

Helen's eyes again brimmed with tears, but this time she didn't leave the room. "You have my condolences on your loss, too."

Knowing the woman meant her mother, Melanie mumbled, "Thanks," hoping she wouldn't have to fabricate some lie.

"I don't know what Father wants!" Martin's heated voice vibrated along her nerves as he escorted his wife into the room. "But he asked us to gather in the study, and gather we shall."

"If he wants this party to come off without a hitch, I need every moment…" Eleanor's words trailed off when she spied Melanie. "What is *she* doing here?" Eleanor asked in a stage whisper. Her lips tightened and she took one of the leather chairs as far away from Melanie as she could get.

What a pleasure to be so well liked. Melanie sighed. At least Helen didn't seem to hate her, after all.

"So where's Grandfather?" Vincent asked, striding into the room. He left one empty seat between him and Melanie.

"Beats me," Melanie said.

"I would have thought you would be keeping better track of him so you could wend your way into his wallet…uh, heart."

Irritated, Melanie sweetly said, "Haven't we had this conversation before?"

Vincent glowered at her. Melanie merely smiled until she heard footsteps along the hall.

Her grandfather's voice boomed into the room. "Ah, good, you're all here."

Accompanied by Andrew, he entered and made straight for his desk. The two men conferred for a moment and Andrew removed some papers from his briefcase.

"Has something terrible happened?" Helen asked.

"No, my dear, I simply have news for you all."

"Did the authorities find John Grey's murderer?" Eleanor guessed.

"Not to my knowledge."

"Then why in the world are we here wasting time when there's so much to do before the party?" Eleanor allowed her pique free rein.

"Because I have an announcement to make that affects you all!" Frederick boomed. "To officially acknowledge my new granddaughter, I've had Andrew draw up some papers and add a codicil to my will."

The room went silent. Melanie felt hostile eyes on her, but she ignored them. Her pulse sped up. She wanted to say she didn't want anything from him— or from any of them—but the truth. Keeping her silence seemed the better choice.

"Andrew, do the honors."

Andrew stated Melanie was to have a trust fund equal to Vincent's, and that, on her grandfather's death, she would get her mother's portion of the estate—a full third—but only if she agreed to claim Slater House as her primary residence and to take her place as a full Slater with all that entailed.

Meaning…letting her grandfather dictate how she was to live her life?

Melanie was stunned speechless.

"This is outrageous!" Martin said. "You're trusting a dead man's word with something so important? How do we even know this woman is Olivia's daughter?"

"Just look at her," Helen said, suddenly coming to Melanie's defense. "It's obvious."

"He's lost it," Eleanor murmured more to herself than anyone else. "His mind really is going."

"Plastic surgery!" Martin was sounding desperate to deny Melanie now. "Grey could have planned the whole thing for a cut of the money."

"Well, he's dead, isn't he," Vincent said. "A corpse will never tell."

"I knew we should have had him evaluated," Eleanor murmured.

Face reddened, Martin pointed a finger at Melanie and asked, "How do we know *she* didn't kill Grey to keep him quiet?"

"How dare you!" Melanie was outraged, unable to keep silent any longer. Her furious glare encompassed Martin and Eleanor and Vincent. "You're so greedy that you accuse me of murder? Take the money and—"

"Good, if you mean it," Eleanor said.

"Enough!" Frederick Slater glowered at them. "The estate is still mine." He softened when he moved toward Melanie and, taking both of her hands in his, pulled her up and out of the chair. "The money is mine to dispense, not theirs, my dear, and I'll divide it however I see fit."

Melanie wanted to say that this wasn't her home, and that she had no intention of living in a nest of vipers, but she swallowed her pride and bit the inside of her cheek to keep herself from doing so.

Her feelings weren't important. Her mother's safety was. And in their minds, she was supposed to be seeking family, not answers that might have consequences for them.

"Thank you for your generosity, Grandfather."

"You're so welcome, my dear."

He pulled her in his arms and hugged her tight. Melanie wanted to push him away, but that would make him suspicious. She had to buy herself enough time to get those answers. Somehow she had to learn the secrets of Slater House. She would get nothing from Martin or his family, that was clear.

But Helen…maybe.

CHANGE OF PLANS. Melanie had to work off some of her anger. She pulled on her jeans, a T-shirt and her orange sneakers and headed for the stables. Riding had always allowed her to work out her feelings and she needed a big dose of that now.

Entering the stable, she came on the same stablehand she'd spoken to the day before, Billy.

"I've decided to explore the estate on horseback," she told him.

"I would suggest Robber Baron for you, miss. Very reliable."

Melanie looked over the horse, a fine specimen if older and quieter than she would like. She needed to let off some steam. Down the shed row, a chestnut whinnied and kicked at the walls of her stall.

"I'll take…" Melanie looked for the horse's name plaque. "Hot Tamale."

"Ah, miss, that's a horse for a very experienced rider."

"Perfect."

Intending to saddle the mare herself, she followed him to the tack room.

"You can just let me have the leathers—"

"And lose my job? *Please*, miss."

Melanie nodded. She didn't want her frustration to affect an innocent bystander.

Billy gathered saddle, pad, bit and reins. She leaned against the doorjamb and let herself be amazed by the tack room. This was no wooden-walled shack but a room as big as her apartment. And better appointed with a skylight above and a cherry-wood floor below. The hooks holding the leathers and bits were all brass.

"We can't ride out together."

The room whirled for a second, but Melanie quickly focused and grabbed on to the past.

"Why not?" I ask. "Who will know? All right, I'll go first and wait for you by the waterfall at the west ridge."

He frowns at me and says, "Someone will figure it out."

A thrill shoots through me and my stomach tightens. "I'm willing to chance it. I just want to spend time with you in the daylight for once."

He cups my face with a callused hand. A hand that does hard work so he can save for college. All the love I feel for him makes me want to shout my joy to the world.

I can't. I don't have that much courage.

Not yet....

"HERE TO MUCK OUT the stalls, Cousin?"

Melanie jerked back to the present to see Vincent staring at her, his expression one of disdain as he surveyed her riding outfit. Dressed in tan jodhpurs, a white polo shirt and black riding boots, he looked very *Town and Country*.

In no mood to play nice, she sweetly said, "If you like, I can shovel some of it your way."

"Don't get too full of yourself, Melanie. You might *think* you have what you came for, but what's to say that can't change in a heartbeat?"

"Change Grandfather's mind? Go ahead."

"Or not. Anything can happen before you become an heiress."

"What? You hope I'll disgrace the family name and he'll disown me?"

He shrugged. "Or you could fall prey to the Slater Curse."

Melanie's pulse threaded unevenly. "That sounds like a threat."

Vincent grinned. "You have an active imagination, Melanie. Must be those movies you make. What reason would I have to threaten you?"

For the second time in one day, she was speechless. Had he really threatened her life or was he just trying to make her afraid enough to leave?

"Hot Tamale is ready, Miss Melanie," Billy called.

Without saying another word, she whipped by Vincent. His gaze stayed with her all the way to the mare—it felt like a sharp knife in her back.

Billy led her just outside, asking, "Do you need a leg up?"

Melanie shook her head. "I can take it from here."

When she'd headed for the stables it had been with no particular plan in mind. But her contact with the past had given her direction.

"How do I get to the waterfall?" she asked as she mounted.

"Which one?"

"West ridge?" She put a question in her voice.

"Up that way." He pointed to a path that would take her through a dense forested area that seemed to go straight up. "That's a pretty tough path. Maybe you'd like to ride out to one of the other waterfalls."

"Another time," she said, squeezing her legs gently.

Hot Tamale took off with a little buck that made Melanie laugh. She was feeling better already. Glancing back at the stable area, she saw Vincent standing, sans mount, staring after her.

Her cousin hadn't come off as a nice guy from the first, but now—bringing up the Slater grandchildren who'd died—he'd given her the creeps.

The sun was shining and the sky was a cerulean blue. The rolling hills around her glowed. Melanie told herself to concentrate on that, on beauty, not on darkness. This would make a fabulous setting for a movie.

A wide shot…a slow pan…

Even so, she couldn't help but feel those eyes in her back, as if Vincent were stalking her. Several times she glanced back but she didn't see any sign of him. Then she was in the forested area and could hardly see anything but green pine needles and leaves.

Hot Tamale was a game mare—though she easily started, she just as easily came back under control. Young and frisky, the mare probably wasn't ridden much. At least it seemed as if she had extra energy to burn. Melanie wondered if she hadn't been Louisa's horse….

Which set her to thinking about the Slater grand-children again. All dead except for Vincent and her, and she was new to the family.

The hills steepened and Melanie leaned a bit over the mare's neck to compensate.

The Slater Curse—could that have something to do with why her mother left?

Had someone tried to kill Mom?

The thought simply jumped into her mind. No one had mentioned murder.

But John Grey had been murdered….

The path became seriously steep and soft between stands of pine. Melanie had to concentrate to keep her seat. She'd never attempted anything like this before. She was practically lying over the mare's neck for balance. Hot Tamale was sure-footed, but every so often the earth moved under her hooves and horse and rider slipped back down a bit, jarring Melanie's stomach to her toes. She didn't even realize how tense she was until they reached the crest and she let go of the breath she'd been holding.

The high spot was flat and covered with pines whose rich scent soothed her. As did the sound of rushing water that told her she was near the west ridge waterfall. No doubt the path through the pines would lead her straight to it.

Excitement curled through Melanie as she wondered if going there would give her another blast from the past. So far, her visions had been tied to the house. But why not out here, as well? The land was part of the estate, after all, she thought as they came to a small clearing along the stream that led to the waterfall.

As she walked Hot Tamale toward the rushing water, she felt the mare's muscles tense up under her legs.

"It's all right, girl," she murmured, patting the side of the mare's neck.

Hot Tamale snorted and settled down.

And Melanie stopped her and stared out toward the rushing water, trying to imagine her mother here.

With Ross? What if he *had* been her mother's boyfriend? Wouldn't that make her own attraction to him inappropriate? Which reminded her that she'd mentioned Mom seeing someone inappropriate and he hadn't said a word.

Just thinking about it made her uncomfortable, so she closed her eyes for a moment and tried to banish the image.

"We can't go on like this."

Melanie tensed, and apparently feeling her stress, Hot Tamale danced sideways.

"Easy, girl, easy."

Forcing herself to relax, Melanie let herself flow into the past.

"I WANT YOU to myself," I say. "Why does everyone have to know about us?"

"It might show that you respect me. That you're not ashamed of me."

"Ashamed? No, I love you."

The words are out of my mouth before I can stop them. They might be true, but telling him might be foolish if it gives him too much power over me.

"Olivia…I would do anything for you. I want you to be mine forever."

He takes me in his arms and presses me close as if he's never going to let me go, and I realize once more he's not into power plays. He's gentle and kind and nothing like the other men in my life.

"That's what I want, too," I say.

"Then let's stop hiding what we feel for each other."

I push him away, torn between my feelings and my fear that Father will ruin this for me. "If you love me, you will wait until I'm ready."

A WHINNY brought Melanie back to the present and she realized they were at the precipice of the waterfall, where rushing water tumbled to a pool thirty feet directly below. The thud of hooves came up fast behind them and Hot Tamale danced in a circle too close to the edge.

Melanie's stomach danced as she tried to get the mare under control.

Horse and rider swooped down on them so lightning-quick that she didn't get a good look before the mare squealed and rose on hind legs, throwing Melanie off balance. Though she fought to stay on, she couldn't. She felt herself flying, propelled straight off the ridge.

The water rushed up and Melanie's stomach dropped faster than the rest of her. Her arms and legs flailed until at last she was caught up in the rushing stream of the waterfall. Her descent slowed a little, but the choppy water tumbled her around. She tried preparing for the shock of landing, tried not to panic.

No time.

She'd barely wondered if the water below was deep enough to protect her from broken bones when she crashed through the surface and plunged into the depths of the pool. Her body jarred against the bottom and her head hit something hard.

Gasping in a combination of water and silt stirred up by the waterfall's power, she imagined the pond tried to hold her in its mucky grip.

No! This wouldn't be her grave!

She fought the lethargy that tried to claim her, fought the roiling water that tried to keep her down. Fought hard. Harder until she exhausted herself.

Surfacing at last, she felt boneless. The bank looked so far away....

Melanie clawed her way toward it. In a last burst of energy that came from some secret place, she grabbed some tall grasses and prayed they would hold and not pull free as she lifted herself out of the water.

Crawling onto solid ground, she collapsed in a puddle...her head aching...her mind drifting.

Chapter Eleven

"Are you okay? Can you answer me?"

Expecting to be confronted by a scene from the past, Melanie opened her eyes to see present-day Ross kneeling over her, his features pulled together in a dark expression.

Her heart thumped against her ribs.

Ross…what is he doing here?

"Does anything hurt?" he asked.

Melanie tested her limbs, then shook her head. Mistake. Too late she remembered hitting something hard at the bottom of the pond.

How long had she been out?

Where had Ross come from?

"Let me help you up."

She stared at his extended hand. "How did you know where to find me?"

"I saw you hit the water."

"How? Why were you out here?"

"I was simply out for a ride just as you were." He shoved his hand closer. "Do you want my help or not?"

"Not."

She rolled away from him, scrambled to her knees and stood.

"Was it something I said?" he asked.

Not knowing why he should have showed up so conveniently, she said, "Maybe it was something you did."

He looked puzzled, then frowned. "You didn't like the way I kissed you?"

Melanie glared at him. Was he for real or was he covering his true intentions?

Someone had used a horse to sideswipe her the way he'd almost done with his car. She tried concentrating, tried to see who had been on that horse, but all she could recall was a dark blur. Her head began to throb and her knees went weak.

"Steady there." Ross gripped her arm and held her upright.

Melanie trembled. Part of her wanted to rip her arm away and run…but part of her said Ross hadn't done a thing wrong.

She gave in and let him help her. "Thanks."

It had to be simple coincidence that had brought them to this place at the same time. He'd ridden here and she'd taken the waterfall express. He couldn't have been on that ridge to knock her off and then gotten here fast enough to help her when she'd surfaced.

Right?

Not unless she'd been out longer than she'd thought. Ross rounded up his horse, a bloodred bay. "If you don't mind riding behind me, I'll have you back at the house in no time and we'll get you a doctor."

"I don't need a doctor."

"You could have a concussion. Let me look into your eyes."

Ross stepped closer and before she knew what he was about, tilted her chin. Thinking he was about to kiss her, Melanie gasped and blinked rapidly. She was about to take a step back when she realized he was trying to judge the size of her pupils. She froze and forced her lids to remain open long enough so he could get a good look.

But the moment he let go of her, she did step back.

"Seems to me your pupils are the same size, but I'm not an expert. You should get a professional opinion."

The way he was staring at her…

An odd chill shot through Melanie and she turned away from Ross. She was thinking clearly and her vision was sharp. All that was wrong with her was a mild headache.

"An ice pack and some aspirin is all I need." She looked up to the top of the waterfall. "Wait! What about Hot Tamale? Who knows where she is?"

"Billy will find her."

Though she wanted to insist they go get the mare—she wanted a chance to see the other horse's hoofprints in the earth—she knew Ross's mount could never make it up a hill that steep with two of them on his back.

"No, not Billy. What if she needs help now?"

"You're certainly in no shape to go wandering around in search of a loose horse."

She couldn't argue with that.

Ross mounted, then took his foot out of the stirrup for her. As she reached for the horse's neck and a handful of mane to steady herself, she was pressed against him. A flash of heat seared her and she was quick to put her left foot in the stirrup and bounce upward. She threw her right leg over the horse's back and circled her arms around Ross's waist.

Trying to ignore her immediate discomfort—now she had double reason—she slipped her foot out of his stirrup and muttered, "Giddyup."

"Nice to know that you still have a sense of humor. Must mean you're basically okay."

But she wasn't okay, not really.

Someone had pushed her over the edge, so to speak!

The question was, did she trust Ross enough to let him know what had happened?

Fairly certain that Ross had been in love with her mother, she was equally certain that she should be able to trust him. He hadn't said he'd seen her fall, but maybe he'd simply been at the wrong angle.

They were halfway back to the stable before she made up her mind and blurted, "I think someone tried to kill me."

"What?"

"Up on the ridge. I didn't take that fall by accident. Someone used a horse to knock into me."

"Why didn't you say something right away? Who?"

Wondering if the villain could have been her cousin Vincent, Melanie said, "I didn't see. I mean I did, sort of. But I was trying to keep Hot Tamale under control as the other horse was on me. It's all a big blur."

She felt Ross stiffen against her arms.

"So you thought I tried to kill you?" He lapsed into silence.

Because she couldn't deny the accusation, guilt rode with Melanie the rest of the way back. Trying to defend herself would simply make things worse. When they dismounted, Billy was nowhere to be seen. But Hot Tamale was standing calmly outside her stall, her hide slicked with sweat.

Melanie was relieved nothing horrible had happened to the mare, after all.

"I'll walk them both out," Ross said. "Are you okay to go inside by yourself? I can take you and—"

"I'm fine. Really."

At least, she was physically okay, other than a slight headache. But knowing someone had tried to harm her...

"You'd better put on some dry clothes before the police come."

Ross's tone was sharp, as if he was irritated, Melanie thought. And his expression was odd.

"No police," she said. "I don't have proof of anything."

And she didn't want the authorities digging into her life. They would easily find her mother was still alive, and that might put Mom back in the line of fire.

"So you're *not* going to make a complaint, put whoever it was on notice?"

"What if I imagined it all? You know…one of my visions of the past spooked me into falling."

"Is that what happened?"

"It could be."

Could, but wasn't. Perhaps telling him had been a mistake even if she did trust him.

"If that's your story."

She nodded. "And I'm sticking to it."

No doctor. No police. No one to raise suspicions and screw up her own investigation.

Turning away from Ross, she headed across the courtyard without looking back. Her nerves were still on edge from the ride back to the stables. If he and her mother had…no, she simply couldn't go there.

Though she wasn't dripping anymore, she was still wet. Good thing there was a mudroom, Melanie thought as she made for the side door.

If only Billy had been around, she would ask him who had taken horses out today. But he wasn't. So she couldn't. Who knew how long he'd been gone— he might not even know.

She was inside the mudroom and slipping out of her orange sneakers when Johnson entered the room and, seeing her, started and dropped one of the riding boots he was carrying.

"My word…Miss Melanie!"

He was so taken aback by her appearance that he didn't even ask what had happened to her.

"I took a little tumble into the water," she explained.

"Apparently."

He was still staring, mouth open. The first time she'd rendered him speechless.

"Well, I think I'll go get dry and change my clothes now. And Johnson, I don't want to worry my grandfather, so if we could keep this between us…"

"Yes, miss, very good."

Sneakers in hand, Melanie left the mudroom and made for the stairs.

So was Vincent back from his ride? No doubt those boots Johnson had been cleaning belonged to her cousin.

What if she faced Vincent? Would he be shocked to see her alive and well?

Melanie really thought about finding him, but in the end she decided she could wait for the pleasure of another confrontation. She was shaky and uncertain and her head was still throbbing a bit. And the skills in obtaining hard-to-get information seemed to have deserted her.

Really, she hadn't even had a shot with people who were so on the defensive.

The new question of the day: Why had someone tried to kill her?

Because he'd guessed what she was up to?

Or because she'd been written into the will? Funny how the attempt had happened barely more than an hour after she'd learned of her good fortune. Perhaps a half hour after Vincent had threatened her.

From now on she would have to be vigilant, would have to watch her own back. Heading home to Chicago would do her no good. Whatever the reason, someone had it out for her, and anyone in this family had enough money to have a long reach.

She had to work fast.

This might be the first time someone tried to kill her, but she wasn't foolish enough to think it would be the last.

ROSS WALKED the horses, felt them to make sure they were cooled down, then watered them, all the while thinking about how Melanie had acted so weird with him.

He tied his horse to a post and led Hot Tamale to her stall. She still seemed a little freaked out and jumped when he removed her tack.

As freaked out as Melanie had seemed, he'd thought he had her where he wanted her. Well, on the way, at least. And now she was pulling back.

It had to be the old man's influence.

Ross wiped Hot Tamale dry. Billy would undoubtedly be back at any time, but Ross's father had been stable master here and Ross had grown up taking care of horses. When he stopped to check the mare's hooves, he found the blood. Her hock was cut, and if he wasn't mistaken, it had been clipped by a flailing hoof.

Evaluating the cut, he didn't think the bleeding was excessive or that the entire thickness of her skin had been penetrated. No debris that he could see.

Fetching the first-aid kit from the tack room, he thought about Melanie. He'd already heard about the codicil—rumors flew along the servant-to-servant underground and in *their* minds he was still one of them.

After cleaning the wound, Ross stopped the trickle of blood by covering the opening with a sterile absorbent pad and wrapped it in place.

Then he saw to his own horse.

So Melanie knew she was in line for a lot of money, but only if she pleased her grandfather. Her being with *him* certainly wouldn't please the old man. But then, he'd been counting on that for leverage.

So why did his plan suddenly irritate the hell out of him?

And why had Melanie taken that step back from him? He'd felt it from the moment she'd opened her eyes.

As if she knew…

When he went back to Hot Tamale, he was pleased to find the bleeding had stopped. The mare was going to need a tetanus booster. In the meantime, he used a wound care ointment on the cut.

And wondered how to repair the tear in his connection to Melanie.

MELANIE SHOWERED and washed her hair, which kicked up the headache that had almost gone away. She took a couple of aspirin and figured if she wasn't okay by the time she was ready to leave the house, she would get that ice pack and wear it into town, where hopefully she would find the elusive Jannie.

But first she was going to call her mother. She still needed to let Mom know about John Grey's murder. Plus she had to know the truth about the role Ross had played in her mother's past. Once the subject of

Slater House was opened, her mother would have to tell her everything.

Wouldn't she?

She tried the cell first. Voice mail. Damn! Then she called the house. The phone rang several times and Melanie was resigned to getting the answering machine when someone answered…in Polish.

"Anna?"

"Ya."

"Melanie," she said, knowing she had to keep it simple for the cleaning lady. "Is my mother there?"

"No missus."

"What time will she be home?"

"Don't know. Gone."

"Gone where?"

"Note no say."

Melanie knew Anna was going to night school to learn English. "Can you read the note to me?"

"Okay, okay!" The sound of shuffling paper was followed by Anna clearing her throat. Then she read haltingly, "'Anna. Need to take…care of…personal matter. Gone for few days.'"

Personal matter…*her*…Melanie was sure of it.

What had happened to playing dead?

"Thank you, Anna."

For the first time since she'd left Chicago, Melanie thought she might have made a really big mistake. In trying to protect her mother, it seemed that she'd placed them both in jeopardy. If only her mother had been straight with her, things wouldn't have gotten out of control.

She was hurrying out the front door as Vincent came in. He recoiled as if he didn't want to get too close. She inspected his face carefully, but he was in control. He merely gave her an insolent expression and pushed his way through.

She turned to glare at him and realized he hadn't changed clothing. He was still wearing his riding outfit, including his boots.

Then whose boots had Johnson been putting back in the mudroom? she wondered.

The thought tweaked her all the way into Slater Corners. Maybe she would simply ask the butler. Now there was a straightforward thought.

She started at the far end of town this time. And rather than playing the good customer, she simply asked the clerks in every store along the street about Jannie. With her mother possibly here already, she didn't have time to waste.

A clerk in a handbag store said, "Oh, Janine doesn't work here. Try down the street at Frivolous Frocks. That's her store."

A break at last. "Thank you!"

Melanie practically ran to the boutique whose windows were filled with what she considered overly fussy dresses—certainly not to *her* taste. Once inside, she looked around the shop decorated in rose and ivory but saw no one who resembled the girl in her memory.

Approaching the nearest clerk—a petite blonde—she said, "Excuse me, but I'm looking for Janine."

"Oh, she's not here today," the blonde said. "But I'd be happy to help you."

"Actually, this is a personal matter. Very important. Can you tell me where she lives?"

The young woman looked at her as though she might be a serial killer. "I'm sorry, miss, but it's against policy to give out an employee's address."

"Then can you call her and tell her I need to speak to her? Please. It's urgent."

"I don't have a number for her. She doesn't have a cell."

"Doesn't she have a telephone at home?"

"Of course, miss, but she's not there. She had to leave town suddenly. Said she'd be back in a few days."

Melanie felt as if she'd been chopped off at the knees. She'd been putting her energy into finding a woman who wasn't to be found. Now what?

"Thanks," she said before leaving the store.

Where had Jannie gone?

Deflated, she headed back to her rental car. She was almost there when she spotted a familiar figure heading into a store.

Helen.

"What the hell," she muttered, thinking she might as well take advantage of the situation, getting the woman alone.

Melanie rushed after her aunt-by-marriage and hurried inside what proved to be a tea shop. Tables covered in lace. Teapots of porcelain and silver and ceramic lining a long shelf. Dozens of glass containers with black and green and herbal loose-leaf teas behind the counter. Melanie hesitated at an old-fashioned, brass-trimmed glass case filled with delectable treats.

Helen was just being seated at a small table with a window view. She looked up, saw Melanie at the door and gave her a tentative smile.

An invitation as far as Melanie was concerned.

She approached Helen and said, "What a coincidence, us running into each other here."

"Would you like to join me?"

Melanie smiled and took the seat opposite Helen. Her mind churned as she tried to figure the best way of getting information out of the woman. She chatted about the shops in town until their steaming pots of tea and a plate of shortbread and lemon curd arrived.

Then Helen suddenly said, "What's on your mind, Melanie? This was no coincidence. You followed me in here, and not because you were in the mood for company."

Grateful that Helen was more astute than she seemed, Melanie said, "You're right. I was hoping you could tell me about my mother. You did know her, right?"

"Olivia was one of my bridesmaids."

"Then you must have known her very well."

"Not really until after I married Nicholas. We did live in the same house."

Wanting Helen to remain in her comfort zone, Melanie knew she had to pace the interview.

She bit a piece of shortbread and sipped at her tea before asking, "What was Mom like back then?"

"Intelligent and spirited. Daring, even. But I'm sure you're aware of that. She had more life and imagination in her than either of her brothers. I loved my dear Nicholas madly, of course, but he was a quiet sort. Intelligent but not adventurous. And Martin…" She shook her head. "Martin talks a good game. In reality, he's ineffectual but he thinks the world owes him. He can be…annoying. Frederick always thought the future of the family rested with Olivia."

Her mother, the hope of the Slater family? Even though she'd experienced some of her mother's memories, Melanie still could hardly believe her mother had been spirited and daring. She'd always seemed so conservative.

Then again, Mom had made her own successes. Perhaps conservative was simply part of the disguise that went with the name Pierce.

"Why do you think Mom ran away from all that?"

"Frederick was so very fond of Olivia—she reminded him of your grandmother, you know. Terrible losing someone you're mad about in the prime of life. At any rate, Frederick put a lot of pressure on Olivia and she was simply too young to deal with it all."

"What kind of pressure?"

"Having to gain entry to an East Coast school… picking her major for her…making her plans for the future." Helen sighed and shook her head. "Frederick wanted the last say in every part of her life."

"Including what men she saw?"

"He tried steering her toward my brother," Helen admitted. "Andrew had the proper breeding, the proper bank account, the proper career, the proper acquaintances. Andrew is the son Frederick always wanted. He's going to back Andrew's campaign for the governor's seat."

"I didn't know your brother was into politics."

"Family tradition," Helen said. "Andrew was fond of Olivia, too. But they weren't right for each other. Olivia was too much of a free spirit. And Andrew has never been much of a ladies' man. Never married," she said, as if she were trying to tell Melanie something without actually saying it.

Too much information, Melanie decided, figuring Andrew's personal life was his own business. Then again, if Andrew really *wasn't* a ladies' man, surely her grandfather had known about it.

"So Grandfather kept pushing them together?"

"Frederick must have figured if he tried hard enough, he would get what he wanted. He was convinced Andrew and Olivia would make the perfect couple."

Though she already knew this part, Melanie asked, "But Mom didn't agree?" as if she had no clue.

"She was seeing someone else in secret."

"Really?"

"Until John Grey saw them together."

Her heart in her throat, Melanie asked, "Who was she seeing?" certain she knew what Helen was going to say.

Helen's pale face flushed with color. "His name was Webb Bennet."

Shocked, Melanie sputtered, "W-Webb?" Not Ross?

"Ross Bennet's older brother. He disappeared the same night as Olivia."

Melanie made the immediate connection. "The reason grandfather tossed the Bennets off the estate."

"So you heard about that."

Melanie's mind whirled. Webb Bennet, not Ross. He and Mom taking off together. What had happened to break them up? she wondered, before a bigger question occurred to her.

Could Webb Bennet be her father? Had Mom been pregnant and Grandfather found out? What had he wanted her to do? End the pregnancy? Was that why Mom had run?

Melanie let her cup drop to the saucer with a clatter.

"I've upset you."

"It doesn't matter. I need to hear the truth. Is there anything more you can tell me?"

Helen's lips pulled into a tight line and Melanie's stomach clenched. She sensed this was the right time to wait and not push. The seconds ticked by and Melanie found herself holding her breath.

"Olivia was frightened," Helen finally said.

Her breath came out in a whoosh. "Of what?"

"I don't know. But I saw her that night. You may not know this, but I lost a child to crib death."

The Slater Curse. "I'm so sorry."

Helen nodded and went on. "I wasn't sleeping much for months after the burial. It was really late and I was out on the terrace getting some air when I saw Olivia running across the grounds."

Melanie practically bit her tongue so she wouldn't interrupt. Her pulse was racing and she could feel her heart pounding.

"She was coming from the south wing, sobbing. At first I thought she'd simply had another fight with Webb. They always seemed to be fighting about something those last few weeks. But Olivia kept looking over her shoulder and then she stumbled. When she went down to her knees, the sounds that came out of her…well, it still gives me gooseflesh. She was terrified. I'm sorry now that I didn't call out to her. I could have helped her. Instead…the next morning…she was gone."

She'd known it! Mom had been in danger—the reason she'd wanted to play dead. But who was it Mom feared? The same person who'd tried to kill her at the waterfall?

"Thank you, Helen. If you think of anything else you can tell me…"

"Maybe some happy stories?"

"That would be wonderful."

Melanie smiled and let Helen talk. She nodded and laughed in all the right places. But her mind was whirling with the pieces of the truth that Helen had revealed.

Mom had been in love with Webb Bennet.

They'd run off together. But if he was indeed her father, why hadn't they stayed together?

She'd only penetrated the tip of the mystery.

HE COULDN'T BELIEVE she'd survived the fall.

He'd had it all so well planned. The moment he'd spotted her going to the stables, he'd known how to get rid of her. Let the Slater Curse be blamed as usual.

Using a branch from a pine tree, he swept the ground, eradicating the proof that another rider had attacked her. He swept his way backward, all the way into a copse of trees.

Damn if Melanie hadn't survived just as had her mother. Two of a kind, those.

He hadn't gone after Olivia himself—he'd made certain arrangements—but the bitch had flown the coop and was certainly on her way here.

He'd had some fast moves to make, certain people to get out of the way long enough to deal with the women who called themselves Pierce.

He was already planning his next moves. Neither Olivia nor Melanie was going to ruin what he'd spent a lifetime building.

Chapter Twelve

Melanie thought to go search for Ross and more answers the moment she got back to the house. But upon arrival, she saw the trucks parked outside of the abandoned wing. Several men were filling a Dumpster while others were loading padded furniture into the back of a van.

So the renovation had begun.

She would have to catch Ross later.

Fearing that her mother had called when she'd been in some no-receive zone, Melanie checked her cell again. No messages. She headed straight for her suite where she was shocked to find Eleanor and a designer-garbed brunette she'd never seen before entrenched in her sitting room.

"Well it's about time," Eleanor said waspishly. "You've kept us waiting long enough."

"For what?"

"For your makeover."

"I don't *need* a makeover."

And not that Eleanor had said a word to warn her about any makeover plans. Undoubtedly, on purpose.

"Whether or not you need a personal shopper is a matter of opinion. Father insisted. He was certain you had nothing suitable for the party he's throwing in your honor."

The damn party!

"Fine." Melanie looked to the brunette. "I'm Melanie."

"Kathryn Godwin."

"So where do we start?"

Kathryn indicated Melanie should follow her into the bedroom. Melanie started off, but when she realized Eleanor wasn't following, she hesitated and cast her aunt a questioning glance.

"Kathryn's taste is impeccable," Eleanor said as she headed in the opposite direction toward the door to the hall. "And I have better things to do."

Just as well, Melanie thought. She didn't need Eleanor overseeing this production.

Melanie entered the bedroom and stopped dead. One end of the room held a couple of portable racks filled with clothing—from the looks of it, undoubtedly none of which would be to her taste. Almost everything on a hanger was white or cream or a pale imitation of a color.

She hated being ambushed like this. But she also needed a dress for the party. And perhaps a few other things to get her by. She hadn't packed much and she wasn't sure how long she would be here.

Pulling the least conservative outfits from the

rack, Melanie picked two sets of crop pants and matching summer-weight sleeveless shells, one in a pale yellow, the other in a bright geranium. Not her taste, but the best she could find from the selection.

"Those will suit you," Kathryn said.

"They'll do."

"Perhaps a day dress?"

"Only if it's backless." Melanie glanced around the room hopefully, as if a rack of more appealing garments might suddenly jump up and surprise her. "Or if it has some kind of interesting detail."

"Sorry, I didn't bring anything like that."

"I'm sorry, too. I'm sure your taste is classic," Melanie said, trying to be tactful, "but there's such a variety in designers today. Don't your younger clients like something a bit more…well, daring?"

"You understand I brought what was dictated by Mr. Slater's orders."

Or by the way Eleanor had interpreted such. "Oh, I understand, all right." Melanie wouldn't put it past the other woman to try to make her as uncomfortable as possible.

As evinced by the cocktail dresses, for example— they reminded her of those frivolous frocks she'd seen in the shop window in Slater Corners.

"This would be my suggestion for the party," Kathryn said.

She pull out a white dress with a full skirt and a high neckline with a heavy border of pearls that would soften any woman's face.

"Very nice for someone else."

"All right. For something different…"

Different was off-white with an even fuller skirt and a deep ruffle around the lower neckline.

"Definitely not me. I'm not getting married." Both those dresses and several others could be used for such. "How about something in red? Chartreuse? Black?" All colors that were missing from the rack.

"Sorry," Kathryn said again.

The woman next chose a pale apricot number, but Melanie reached past her for a gown in a sea blue that reminded her of what her mother had worn in one of the photos she'd seen in the stairwell. It was slim and cut on the bias to hug her figure. And the neckline was fairly low with a line of crystals running around the edge and forming thin spaghetti straps.

Wondering how something so different had made the cut, Melanie said, "This will do."

"Wonderful." Although she appeared a bit puzzled as she studied the dress, Kathryn sounded relieved. "I have a top that would be perfect with it. That dress will be wonderful with your coloring. And your eyes," Kathryn said, though she was frowning at Melanie's hair.

The magenta stripes, no doubt. Resigned that they would have to go, Melanie sighed. Apparently there was no room for individual taste at Slater House. One of many reasons she would never fit in here.

Kathryn handed her a see-through shrug seeded with crystals. Very nice, though it would make the dress more modest.

"Fine," Melanie said, although she wasn't certain

she would wear it. The dress would do fine on its own. "You can leave these few things and take the rest."

"That's it? But I was led to understand you needed an entire wardrobe."

"Then you were misled."

"Well, all right. But you need to try on the pieces you chose for possible alteration."

"I'm sure they'll fit." Heading for the door, Melanie said, "Just leave them and I'll try them on."

Thinking she heard a shocked gasp from behind her, Melanie smiled as she sailed out of the room and headed for the south wing. There had to be a entrance from this level and she intended to find it.

She passed mostly what she assumed were suites with closed doors. A couple of sitting rooms. A very male den with leather club chairs around a fireplace. At the end of the hall, she came to a small conservatory filled with ferns and hanging plants and a seating arrangement overlooking the gardens. Several large screens painted with garden scenes were placed around the room. But no door to the south wing.

Or was there?

Looking out the window, she could see the garden side of the abandoned wing—it overlapped the conservatory. Then she realized one of the decorative screens served a practical purpose.

Melanie slipped behind the screen and saw the closed doors. Great. They were probably locked. She tried a handle anyway, and to her surprise heard the catch click just before the door creaked open.

She slipped through and into the abandoned wing,

then stopped to let her eyes adjust. No lights on up here. Though she wondered if they worked, she chose not to try the wall switch. Noises still came from the floor below, so the workers apparently hadn't yet left. She hoped to wander around up here in peace and not be interrupted, which she was certain would happen if she alerted Ross to her presence. While she wanted to talk to him, she first would see if the walls up here would talk to her.

The second floor of the abandoned wing seemed to be in keeping with the main house. A series of suites—sitting room, bedroom, bath. Day rooms with seating arrangements facing the windows or around fireplaces. The furniture was mostly intact, albeit loaded with dust and bits of plaster and other materials the rooms had shed. The ceiling looked ready to cave in places, and parts of the walls had.

She kept trying to picture her mother in one room and then another, but nothing came to her. No visions. No voices. Not even an instinct that her mother had ever been in one of these rooms before...

Not until she got to the end of the corridor and the big open area above the ballroom.

"Aa-aa-ah!"

The scream rang in Melanie's head. But it sounded so real, so immediate, she whirled around, heart pounding, trying to figure out from where the sound had come. The floor beneath her foot groaned, making her jump.

Suddenly fear gripped her like a fist around her middle and wouldn't let go. Her head went light but this time something in her fought giving in to it. She tried to relax, to go with the flow of the past, but she simply couldn't.

Or was it the past calling her?

Had she heard a *real* scream?

"Mom?" she called, her fear tangible. "Are you here?"

"What the hell?"

Melanie whirled around to find Ross directly behind her. Her heart was beating fast, her breath nearly nonexistent. She took a step toward him…reaching…her head growing light at last…

He helped her to a small sofa. Her legs shook as she sat and as dust rose around her in a cloud, she sneezed.

"How did you get past me?" Ross asked, sitting next to her, so close that his knee pressed into hers.

"Second floor door from the main house."

"Impossible. It's locked."

"Not."

Too close to Ross for her comfort after what Helen had told her, Melanie tried squeezing herself into the corner. Still, their knees touched.

"Huh. Frederick locked those doors himself after Louisa died in here," Ross told her. "Why would anyone unlock them?"

"You're asking the wrong person about that." Melanie took a deep, steadying breath. "Maybe Grandfather unlocked it himself so he could come in here and look down on the spot where his granddaughter died. Maybe the Slater Curse haunts him."

Maybe that was what was haunting her.

"So what the hell happened?" Ross asked.

"I was a little out of it…. There was a scream…." Unsure if she'd remembered or heard the piercing sound, she said, "You tell me."

"I didn't hear any scream. I arrived just as you called out for Olivia. I'm assuming you must have been coming out of a memory."

"No. I don't think so. I heard a scream and—"

"Thought you heard your mother?"

Melanie nodded. "But that's it. It was like an echo…distant…warning me. Maybe it was from the past. But something stopped me from remembering."

Ross leaned closer and cupped her cheek. "This has got to be hell on you."

It *was* hell, especially with him so close. Especially now because Mom had gone missing. Melanie not only had to find out what had happened in the past, she had the immediate present to worry about. Talking about it might make her feel better, but she couldn't even be honest about it with Ross. As far as he was concerned, her mother was dead.

But there was something she could talk about, something she could get straight with him. "Why didn't you tell me that my mother and your brother were close?"

Ross's eyebrows arched, dark slashes over eyes that were a muddy green in the fading light.

"Why didn't you tell me you knew?" he asked.

"I just heard it this morning from Helen, actually. I can't believe you didn't even tell me you have a brother."

"Had," Ross said, getting to his feet. "I haven't heard from him in twenty-five years."

There it was, her opening.

"What happened, Ross? Why did Mom run? And if she and Webb ran together…"

"I don't think they did."

"Everyone else does…why not you?"

"Webb would never have abandoned Olivia."

"Then what happened to him?"

Something flickered over Ross's face…some…knowledge of some sort. For a moment she thought she was going to get her answer.

"Hell if I know." Ross sighed. "If he went after Olivia and she turned him away, he would've come home. Or at least he would have called me to let me know where he was. He never did, never in twenty-five years."

"Wait a minute. You didn't even know that they weren't together until I showed up. What made you think they didn't leave together?"

"Olivia had broken up with Webb. That's why I think she left alone. And if she did and Webb went after her, I'm not sure how he would have found her."

"Then maybe he had to disappear just like Mom did," Melanie said. "Maybe he's out there somewhere in hiding. What in the world could have happened to drive them both away from this place for good?"

There was silence between them for a moment, and Melanie's mind whirled. This mystery became more complicated by the hour. At least she'd garnered some new knowledge, although not anything she'd wanted to face. So Webb Bennet was her biological father, making Ross...

Someone she shouldn't be attracted to.

Thankfully she hadn't let the attraction get out of hand. Some little comfort when she suddenly felt so miserable.

"Maybe you should get the picture and get out while you can," Ross suddenly said. "If she were alive, Olivia would probably hate that you've come back in her stead."

Guilt surged through Melanie. Mom was alive, of course, and she did hate it. She'd hated it so much that she'd risked herself by coming after her daughter. Not that Melanie was going to volunteer that information any more than Ross had volunteered the information about his brother.

"I'm not leaving until I learn the truth."

"Why become obsessed with ancient history?"

"*My* history."

"Olivia's."

"But she *is* my mother."

The present tense "is" slipped easily from her lips, but thankfully, Ross didn't seem to notice.

"And apparently she didn't want you to know why she wasn't happy here." He moved closer to her. "She was too much like you."

"Which means?"

"Strong, smart, unconventional. A little bullheaded. What did you think I meant?"

The breath caught in her throat once more. And once more she had the feeling that he was going to kiss her. He moved in, leaving her nowhere to go. Trying not to panic, she shoved a hand in his chest and pushed.

Ross grinned at her. "Do I really make you that nervous?"

"Hell, yes...*Uncle Ross*..."

"Uncle?" A wide-eyed Ross began to laugh.

"You think it's funny?"

Still grinning, Ross shook his head. "We're not related, so relax."

A weight lifted from her even as she shook her head. "Webb is my father, right?"

"I'm afraid not, Melanie."

"What do you mean? If Mom loved him—"

"And Webb loved her."

"Then how do you know she wasn't pregnant with me when she left here?"

"I didn't say she wasn't pregnant, just that Webb wasn't your father."

Another silence. Stunned, Melanie thought she heard the ticking of a clock somewhere, then realized it was her own heartbeat.

"I don't understand. So there *was* a Larry Pierce?"

"For all I know."

"What *do* you know?"

Ross sighed and moved away from her. "You just won't leave it alone, will you? I told you Olivia broke it off with Webb. He tried to find out why and they fought like crazy."

"Helen said they were arguing...."

"Then one morning I went for a ride and found

Olivia on the trail. She was on her knees, throwing up. I was a little in love with her myself and I panicked. I mean, I was just a kid—twelve—so what did I know? Anyway, I thought maybe she was dying and told her I would go for help, get a doctor. She wouldn't let me. She swore me to secrecy and I guess she took the secret to her grave." Ross shook his head. "Olivia told me she was pregnant, but that it wasn't Webb's and *that's* why she broke it off with my brother."

"What?"

How could that be? Her mother had dated a lot of men over the years, but only one at a time. And she'd loved Webb.

This made no sense.

"How do you know she wasn't lying?" Melanie asked.

"Because I didn't believe her about it not being Webb's baby. Despite my promise to Olivia, I went to my brother, told him that he needed to be a man and own up to his responsibility. He swore he'd never slept with Olivia and he seemed so crushed and angry that I believed him. And that was the last I saw of either of them."

Melanie tried to absorb it all. "If your brother didn't get Mom pregnant, then who? Was she close to any other man?"

"Other than Frederick?"

"I meant romantically. Andrew?"

He shook his head. "Andrew was too civilized for the likes of Olivia. But Roger Johnson wasn't."

"The butler?"

"The same. Of course, Roger's father was the butler then. Roger had been away at college, but he'd graduated and was at loose ends. We always thought he and Jannie would get together, but something didn't go right there and Olivia seemed to be willing to console him."

Or maybe Mom was the reason the other couple had split? Melanie couldn't believe no one else had noticed if this were true. But surely her grandfather didn't know or Johnson wouldn't be his butler now.

"Janine Marsh seems to be the key to everything," Melanie said. "Too bad she's missing in action or maybe we could get her to spill."

"You tried to find her?"

Melanie nodded. "Apparently she's left town temporarily."

"Huh."

"It seems like something…or someone…is trying to keep me from the truth."

"What? You think someone paid Jannie Marsh to leave town for a while?"

"It's a possibility. The thing is, what if I decided to stay? Would she never return?"

"Maybe whoever got her to leave is counting on your leaving, as well."

"Or dying…." She hadn't forgotten how close she'd come to drowning. "Maybe the Slater Curse isn't a curse, after all," she mused. "Maybe it's being orchestrated."

"Multiple murders?"

"Don't you find it awfully convenient that—until Grey found me—Vincent was the only Slater grandchild to stay alive?"

"You're accusing him?"

"I'm not accusing anyone. I'm just saying…"

"Both Martin and Eleanor are grasping…but murder?"

"Someone tried to kill me at the waterfall. Someone who has a stake in the Slater fortune."

"I thought you imagined it," he said, reminding her of the story she'd used to avoid making a formal complaint to the authorities.

"I only wish I had."

Ross took her in his arms and held her close, making Melanie feel safer than she had in what felt like aeons rather than mere days. His chest was pressed against hers and she could feel the rapid drill of his heart. His breath ruffled her hair and she felt him touch his lips to her forehead.

He was about to kiss her—she knew it—when a sharp whistle shattered the moment.

"Hey, boss, you up there?" a man shouted. "We need you down here to make some decisions about what stays and what goes."

"Be right down," he called, then brushed Melanie's lips with his. "We'll continue this conversation later. In the meantime, lock the doors to your suite and try to stay out of trouble."

Melanie would have returned the salvo if she only could have thought of a clever answer. But truth be told, Ross was right. No sense in taking un-necessary chances.

She put her fingers to her lips. He'd kissed her so softly…not like a man who'd wanted something from her but one who'd wanted to reassure her. One who cared.

Was it possible in such a short time?

Warmth filled her and she had a sudden sense of well-being that no other man had given her. How? When her world was so crazy, her future so uncertain.

She'd never felt…this…before…but she sus-pected she might be falling in love with Ross Bennet.

The question was, did he have true feelings for her or was she simply an extension of her mother for him? He'd been in love with Mom. He'd said so. He might only have been a kid, but he'd never worried, so how did she know he wasn't still carrying a torch?

And where did that leave her?

HERE AT LAST. Olivia turned the car into a pullover right after the blind curve and cut her engine. She could turn the car around and drive out without any-one the wiser.

As soon as she got Melanie to come with her.

She stopped for a moment to get her bearings. The hulk of Slater House lay below. It was the dead of night and tendrils of fog embraced the structure, making it look as evil as she remembered it to be.

Though she was exhausted, a single-minded pur-pose drove Olivia and she hurried down the path to the north of the house. She should have been here this morning—and would have if she hadn't had that blowout on the road. Luckily, she had great reflexes and had wrested the car to the pullover. She could easily have been killed....

Not the only time in her life that she'd faced death and survived.

She stayed out of sight under cover of a stand of trees as she approached the stable. One of the horses wickered softly. For a moment she grew nostalgic, but then she remembered why she had left this house of horror.

And soon she would be gone again, never to return.

It had taken forever to get a tow in the middle of nowhere. Then she'd had to wait until morning to get a new tire. Her spare was one of those minis, fine for getting someplace safe but not for driving hundreds of miles. Having gotten a room at the local motel, she'd overslept and hadn't gotten back onto the road until midafternoon.

Maybe later was better. Before anyone could stop her, she could get Melanie to safety under cover of night.

She rounded the stables and used the terrace stairs, stopping at the door to her old rooms. Stooping, she detached the loose stone from the wall. She'd hidden a key that had been useful when she'd sneaked out at night for a midnight rendezvous.

The key wasn't here.

Damn! Now how was she going to get in? The servants had always been careful to lock up at night.

Even so, she moved along the terrace, trying

doors. All locked. Now what? Break a window? She couldn't be certain the estate hadn't been wired to some security system. Then it came to her. The answer was right before her eyes.

The abandoned wing....

Hurrying, she tried the closest door, but it, too, was locked. Her need to get inside and find her daughter grew. She had the weirdest sensation.

Instinct made her look around to make sure no one was watching.

No one that she could see....

Her breath was coming in quick spurts, her pulse racing as she rounded the wing, tried every door until she got to one that was unlocked. Slipping inside, she let go a sigh of relief.

But her relief was short-lived when she stepped away from the door and nearby footfall told her she wasn't alone.

Heart thudding, she stopped to listen, to determine where the sound had originated. Nothing. Hoping she'd imagined it, she started off again toward the foyer and the doorway on the other side that would lead her to the main house.

Suddenly the doorway was blocked, the impediment in shadow. Even so, she recognized him. Her heart pounded. All her fears had been justified.

"It's about time, Olivia," he said. "I've been waiting for you."

Chapter Thirteen

After a restless sleep, Melanie was determined that she had no time to waste. She would make every waking moment count in pursuit of the truth.

Before she left her room, she checked her cell to see if she'd missed any calls. No. Then she tried calling Mom's cell in hopes that her mother would actually answer. Strike two.

"Here goes nothing," she muttered, setting off for the stables.

When she walked in, Billy was measuring out feed for the horses.

"Morning, miss. Ready to take another ride?"

"No, not today. I just wanted to check on Hot Tamale, make sure she was okay."

"Why wouldn't she be?"

"No reason." Apparently he hadn't a clue as to what had happened to her. "Just an excuse for a visit."

"There's some carrots over there if you want to give her some."

"I'd love to." Melanie fetched the treat and gave

it to the mare. "So who all went riding yesterday morning?"

Billy shrugged. "I wasn't here the whole time. Had to go into town for some supplies that seem to be misplaced. Vincent went out right after you. But when I got back, I noticed Johnson's horse was a bit lathered, so he must have gone out, as well."

"Johnson has a horse?"

"Dream By Night."

"I didn't even know he rode."

"Everyone who's spent any time on the place does, and Johnson was born on the estate."

There was something in Billy's tone. "I get the feeling you don't exactly like Johnson."

"He acts like he's family rather than being one of us. You know, like he's entitled."

Melanie hadn't noticed, but then Johnson probably showed a different face to the other workers than he did to the family. So why would he feel entitled? Because he was the butler? Or because he'd gotten close to her mother? Melanie simply didn't know whether or not to believe the man could be her biological father.

"So I take it you weren't born on the place, Billy."

"Not me. Been working here since I was in high school, though."

Which, if his looks were a true indicator, was longer than twenty-five years.

"Someone told me that when he got out of college, Johnson was involved with one of the maids," Melanie said. "He didn't marry her, did he?"

"Jannie? He dumped her. He had higher aspirations. Got real friendly-like with Miss Olivia, if you'll forgive my saying so."

"Really? You mean, they had a romance?"

"I can't say for sure, but Miss Olivia was always real nice to Johnson."

"You seem to have known her pretty well yourself."

"She was a spirited rider, that one. Like you, I guess."

"Did Johnson ever marry?"

"Years ago. Didn't last long, though."

Melanie nodded. "You wouldn't know why my mother ran away from Slater House, would you?"

"No. Sorry."

But Melanie could see that something was bothering him.

"I just wish I knew more about my mother's past. I hate to think of her as being so unhappy."

"She wasn't, not until those last couple weeks. To tell you the truth, she was a changed girl."

"And you have no idea of what happened?"

"I'd say you'd have to ask Mr. Frederick about that," Billy said.

Making her think that her grandfather knew something significant about her mother's mind-set when she'd taken off from Slater House. Maybe Billy, too, though he'd neatly avoided her direct question.

Melanie thought about the stablehand's assessment of Johnson all the way back to the house.

A sense of entitlement. Why? Because he was the butler? Or because he'd slept with her mother? Did he know Mom had been pregnant?

Did Roger Johnson wonder if she, Melanie, was his daughter?

The more she dug, the more questions she had.

Entering the house, Melanie was on the lookout for the butler. She wanted to get close up and personal to see if there was anything in his face reflected in her own.

But to her chagrin, the only person waiting for her was Eleanor. And from the look on *her* face…

"You'll need to hurry and get changed."

"Changed for what?"

"Oh, don't argue, Melanie. I don't like this any more than you do. I'm only trying to please Frederick. Once I deliver you, I have a dozen errands to run for the party."

"Deliver me to where?"

"Just change. One of the new outfits, please."

Sighing, Melanie hurried up the stairs to her quarters. Better to do it, get it over with, than to argue with Eleanor.

Ten minutes later, dressed in the yellow outfit, Melanie was in Eleanor's BMW.

Deciding that pussyfooting around had been getting her nowhere, she asked, "Did you hate my mother, too?"

"Hate Olivia? Of course not. She could be rude and unthinking at times, but then, most teenagers are."

"Then it's just me."

"I don't know you well enough to hate you."

"You do a great imitation, then."

Silence ticked between them for a moment before Eleanor said, "You have to understand how difficult it's been for me, trying to be a Slater. I've had to fight for Frederick's acceptance. And then you waltz in, the spitting image of Frederick's precious Olivia and you automatically go to the head of the line."

"What line? I'm not trying to take anything away from you or yours, Eleanor. I don't know that I want anything but the things I missed out on that matter to a kid. A family. A sense of belonging." Surprised at herself—Melanie had always thought Mom was enough for her—she was being honest. "You should be able to relate to that."

Eleanor didn't agree. She didn't say anything. Melanie wondered if there was a way to get something useful out of the woman when she pulled the car into a lot.

"We're here and almost on time."

"Okay, on time for what?"

"Your transformation."

A transformation that was going to take place at a day spa called Leading Lady, which made Melanie think of the movies. Somehow she couldn't get into the image of her as a star. More like the next victim in a murder mystery.

Only if she didn't do something to save herself, Melanie decided. She couldn't just go around forever asking questions. She needed to act, to force the would-be killer's hand.

Maybe then everything would fall into place and she would at last have all the answers she had come to Slater House to find.

A plan took root in her mind….

SATISFIED the renovation was on its way at last, Ross settled into the room overlooking the gardens that he'd chosen to make his office. He'd had the movers bring in a magnificent cherrywood desk and a leather-and-cherrywood chair from an upper room. He'd found a leather couch, as well, which he'd had set in front of the fireplace. And a leather chaise near the windows. A couple of mahogany side tables and lamps finished the room. The only thing he'd brought in from the outside was a drawing board on which he was spreading the blueprints.

So much to do. He'd sent out much of the furniture and area rugs to temporary storage and the rest was waiting in the ballroom for removal on Monday. All couches and chairs would be reupholstered. Wooden furniture needed to be refinished to bring back the original beauty. The rugs had to be professionally cleaned.

But all that could wait.

The actual structure needed a lot of repair, and with the furnishings stripped, he could see how much work that would entail.

He got busy going over his notes, trying to prioritize, but he was having trouble settling down.

"So here you are."

Ross snapped around to see the lord of the manor standing in the doorway, staring at him as if he were sizing up his competition.

"Frederick, where else would I be?"

The old man looked around the room as he entered

and sat on the couch arm. "Made yourself comfortable, have you?"

"I figure I'll be working here long enough to need a base for the renovation."

"Just don't get *too* comfortable."

A few seconds ticked by during which Ross quickly analyzed Frederick's intentions. This was the first time he'd come to the south wing since going to contract with Ross. Well, as far as Ross knew. They hadn't done a walk-through together and he hadn't come to see what was going on. Frederick had told him the decisions as to what needed to be done were his, and that had been that.

So why was he here now?

Melanie, of course.

"Too comfortable?" Ross finally repeated in the form of a question.

"Stay away from my granddaughter."

"Well, that's certainly direct."

"You're hired help and she's family. Remember that."

"No, Frederick, you remember that I'm not on your payroll. I'm not a servant. I'm a legitimate businessman. You might be able to order me off your property, but you won't get out of an ironclad contract."

Frederick looked at him assessingly. "What is it you want to stay away from her?"

Not that he wanted to stay away from Melanie, Ross answered, "The truth would be refreshing."

"*Which* truth?"

How many were there? Ross wondered. How many secrets in this house?

"What did you do to Webb?"

"What will the truth get me?"

"Always the negotiator. Depends."

"Stay away from my granddaughter."

"How about I don't turn her against you."

"You don't have the chops."

"Try me."

Frederick sized him up for a moment before saying, "You're as arrogant as your brother was."

"So you warned him off Olivia?"

"I offered him a small fortune to stay away from her, enough for him to start his own architectural firm. Not that he considered it. He wouldn't take a penny. Made me respect him until they ran away together."

"You're sure that's what happened."

"I'll tell you what I'm sure of, Ross. You can have all the contracts in the world, but that won't protect you from someone with my money and connections. I can buy anyone to do anything. So don't piss me off!"

With that, Frederick left, leaving Ross a little stunned. The old man had threatened him. Damn, he hadn't expected that! It left a sour taste in his mouth, made him wonder what Frederick Slater might do to get his own way. Made him wonder if the old man hadn't done something to stop Webb….

Frederick Slater had been responsible for Ross's father turning to drink—a situation that eventually killed him—and for his grandfather's heart being broken, because they'd lost not only their home but their way of life. It hadn't been a personal act of vengeance.

Not in the way Frederick had just threatened him, Ross thought, having no doubt the old man was capable of doing anything to get what he wanted.

Suddenly it hit him what Frederick hadn't brought up in their argument. If the old man truly thought Webb was Melanie's father, it wouldn't get past him that Ross would be her uncle. But Frederick hadn't verbalized that connection. Had he missed it—Ross had noticed that at times, the old man wasn't quite functioning on all cylinders anymore—or did he know the truth about Melanie's parentage?

Whichever, Ross wasn't giving in to threats.

He tried to get back to work, but thoughts of Melanie kept intruding.

Leaning back in his chair, he wondered what he was going to do about the woman. In some ways, she was a thorn in his side. He didn't need the feelings she stirred in him, that was for damn certain. That made her a distraction, one he couldn't afford. He couldn't afford to have anything go wrong with this project.

Or with his own search for the truth.

He'd played the cards he held to learn what Frederick knew, but in the end—assuming the old man had been honest—Ross wasn't any closer to the truth then he had been before.

What was he going to do now? He was desperate.

Guilt had been eating at him for years. He'd suppressed the debilitating emotion long enough. It was time to face his fears full-on.

Ross had to know whether Webb was alive, and if not, whether he'd caused his own brother's death.

FOR SEVERAL HOURS Melanie allowed herself to be massaged, glowed, manicured and pedicured. A facial was followed by a session with a hair colorist who—big surprise—eradicated any trace of magenta from the red before a stylist took over and cut and blow-dried her hair. Melanie insisted on her favorite hairstyle, however, hair pulled back into a twist fastened with chopsticks. She wanted to be able to recognize something about herself.

But when the cosmetologist made up her face so skillfully that it looked almost natural, Melanie really didn't recognize herself. She felt as if her mother was staring at her out of the mirror. A young Mom, looking as she had when she'd still lived at Slater House.

The thought sent a shiver up Melanie's spine.

As if her radar were in perfect tune, Eleanor showed up just then to take her home, but not before one of the consultants handed her a bag filled with skin care items and makeup.

All this was just temporary, Melanie thought as she got into the car. Once she was home in Chicago, she would be free to be herself again.

"You look presentable," Eleanor said begrudgingly.

"You mean, you hope I won't embarrass you tomorrow."

"That would be smart of you."

"Smart how?"

What did Eleanor think would happen to her if she didn't conform to her grandfather's wishes.

Not that Eleanor answered.

The drive to Slater House was fast, and once they arrived, her aunt let Melanie off at the front door before zooming away again.

Free at last. Thinking she could do some more exploring, Melanie entered the house. The first person she ran into was her grandfather.

He stopped and stared at her and his voice grew gruff. "You're so like her," he murmured, placing his hands on her shoulders. "It's as if I have her back again."

Melanie stiffened and then forced herself to relax. He was her grandfather, after all. He might have done things wrong with her mother, but he'd been punished by her absence. And now he was an old man.

"I'm not my mother," she reminded him.

His eyes were watery and his forehead pulled into a frown. "Olivia, too, though I was really thinking of my dear Mildred."

Her grandmother, who'd died too young. For a moment her heart went out to the man who'd lived nearly three decades without the love of his life. Then realizing he was still holding on to her arms possessively, his fingers digging into her flesh, she grew uncomfortable and broke free.

"It's obvious you loved my mother. What happened, Grandfather? What happened to make her run away?"

"It was that Bennet boy. He took her away from me."

"You mean Webb? How do you know she left with him? Did you see them together?"

"I was asleep at the time. Coward that he was, Webb stole Olivia in the middle of the night."

"If you were asleep, then how do you know what happened?"

"Because I'm not a fool, my dear. They were both gone in the morning."

"Maybe they left separately," Melanie argued. "Mom broke up with Webb, so maybe he simply decided he couldn't be around her any longer."

"Only one car was gone. Olivia's, of course, because it was a BMW."

He spoke as if Webb were after the Slater money. If so, he'd gone about it in completely the wrong way. And Melanie was certain her grandfather had realized that.

"Did you really hate Webb Bennet so much?"

"He betrayed me. I can't abide disloyalty."

Exactly why Johnson had said her grandfather had fired Janine Marsh.

Melanie wondered how little it took to be disloyal in her grandfather's mind, but she figured she dared not ask. She needed to play her part for a while longer.

He cleared his throat. "About your escort for tomorrow night...I've picked a suitable young man—"

"No need to worry about that," Melanie quickly interrupted. "I already have an escort."

Her grandfather's expression darkened. "Don't tell me you're going with Ross Bennet."

Had he noticed the attraction between them or had someone else been bending his ear? she wondered.

Feeling his disapproval like a tangible thing, she knew Ross would not be her right choice. Not if she wanted her grandfather to be open with her. For him to do that, she had to stay on his good side.

"No, not Ross," she said. "Andrew."

Her grandfather's visage cleared in an instant. "Ah, Andrew. You could do worse. A fine young man. Upstanding. Successful. He's going to go far in politics, you mark my words."

Andrew wasn't exactly young, but she guessed he was to someone her grandfather's age. "Helen said you're going to back his campaign for the governor's seat."

"You and Andrew will make a fine couple, Olivia."

Olivia?

"Grandfather, I'm Melanie."

Confusion flicked across his face. Then he said, "Of course you are," and walked away.

Leaving a troubled Melanie staring after him.

Why had he called her by her mother's name? Had it been a simple slip of the tongue? Or was something else slipping—like her grandfather's mind?

Maybe it was living in this house with its curse and ghosts. She'd only been here for less than a week and already she felt haunted.

And more afraid than she might have imagined possible.

Had someone tried to kill her for the money...because whoever it was knew she was searching for the truth…or simply because she looked so much like her mother?

Had the attempt been motivated by greed or by an unbalanced mind?

Melanie needed the answer and fast. And she could only think of one way of getting it.

Her mother's memories.

She had to go back to the abandoned wing when no one was around and face down her fears.

Chapter Fourteen

Melanie waited until long after dark before venturing back into the abandoned wing. No amount of phone calls to Mom's cell had brought the woman to the phone. Melanie was scared for her. She talked to her mother on a daily basis. Mom would know she'd be going nuts with worry by now. She would have gotten a message to her somehow. Something must have happened or Mom would already have arrived.

Or maybe she had.

Melanie prayed Mom was okay.

But where the hell could she be? Melanie felt as though she was going to burst before she found out.

The inside of the house was quiet, but outside a storm seemed to be brewing. Wind whipped the trees and every so often sent some loose object skittering against the building.

Her imagination engaged, Melanie swore the walls around her breathed as if the house were some alive entity. But undoubtedly she was just hearing her own breath just as she heard her own heartbeat.

And surely that wasn't a scuffle behind her but some debris crashing against the outer wall.

She stopped to listen…*nothing*…but she sensed something…*her mother?*…then went on to the open area where she'd heard the scream. A memory that pebbled the flesh on her arms and set the fine hairs along the back of her neck at attention.

That scream still haunted Melanie.

Determined to find its source, she stopped in the middle of the second-floor hallway. Closing her eyes, Melanie listened hard. Could her mother be here now? She sensed Mom…but was it in the present or the past? Melanie couldn't pin down her presence. She concentrated on finding any link at all to her mother.

Her breath slowed but suddenly her pulse shot up with a jolt and everything shifted in a heartbeat.

She felt physically thrown across the room.

Opening her eyes, Melanie saw nothing in the shadows, but she felt it—fear—and suddenly she was the one screaming….

I SCREAM AS I run, but before I can get away, he grabs me from behind and pulls me into a room. I fight, elbows flailing, heels kicking back, but a blow to my head sends me reeling.

Suddenly I find myself flat on my back on a couch, my skirts up to my waist. I try to push him away, to get out from under him, but he's too strong.

"I'll teach you to defy me!" he growls at me.

Horrified, I scream again and fight with all my might. I turn my hands into claws and go for his

face, but he merely ducks and grabs both my wrists.
With one hand he pulls them above my head, with his
other hand, he rips my panties.

I feel his fingers probing between my thighs....

WITH A CRY, Melanie pulled herself out of the past
before she could remember the details of her
mother's violation.

Her heart was thundering, her pulse rushing
through her ears so hard that she nearly missed the
footfall somewhere behind her. Whipping around,
still a little confused by the terrible truth she'd begun
to remember, she searched the shadows.

Nothing…and then movement.

He was coming after her…now…in the present!

Flight instincts kicking in, she ran. She heard him
behind her, following. Glancing over her shoulder,
she saw the shadows move once more, all it took to
urge her faster. She flew down the hall, her only
thought to get out via the staircase down into the
ballroom.

Terror made her clumsy.

Her shoulder hit the wall and she stumbled forward, her foot landing hard. The sound of splinter-
ing wood beneath it crawled up her spine.

Tripped by damaged floorboards, she went down
hard but reached out to stop her fall. Her hands hit
the ground as the wood hit by her knees gave with
an explosive crack. Her body jerked downward, first
through the floor, then through the ceiling below.
She grabbed for a hold, her grip slip…slip…slip-

ping… until she was stretched out, hanging over the ballroom, unable to see what lay below in the dark.

A shadow loomed over her…she could hear his low laughter. Dry lightning lit the windows, casting a blue glow around his distorted form. And then she saw his leg stretch out and his foot come down toward one of her hands that still hung on for dear life.

Before the foot could smash Melanie's hand, reflex made her let go and suddenly she was hurtling downward, her heart and stomach dropping faster than the speed of light.

Knowing the ballroom floor was rushing up to meet her, she braced for the impact. But when she jolted to a stop, her landing was soft—upholstered furniture and rolled rugs apparently waiting for removal broke her fall. Still, her knees crumpled and she crashed down on one hip. Then her landing pad shifted and she tumbled from plaster-dusty cushions onto the hard floor.

Stunned but unharmed, Melanie scrambled to get her legs under her. How long did she have until the bastard caught up to her? Before she could find her feet, sconces along the wall illuminated the long room with soft light.

"What the hell is going on?"

Melanie nearly melted down when she saw it was Ross. "Thank God, it's you."

"Are you all right? What happened?"

"Nothing broken. Not on me. But the floor…"

She pointed to the ceiling and the hole she'd dropped through.

"What the…? How did I miss that?"

"I don't know. Just get me out of here." She would tell him everything as soon as she caught her breath.

Melanie took a step, but her knee buckled. Ross caught her, then before she could stop him, he swung her up into his arms.

"I can walk," she insisted.

"Save it."

There was no use in arguing with him, so Melanie simply hung on and swept her gaze over the length and breadth of the ballroom. Not that there was anything to see. Whoever had tried to kill her was undoubtedly long gone.

Then the newest memory stirred in her mind and she felt as if she were going to be sick. For her current documentary, she'd interviewed countless women who'd been abused by men in one way or another. The one woman she'd never thought to interview was her own mother.

The connection between her real life and her reel life put her in emotional turmoil. No longer was she the filmmaker with distance between her and her subject. She was living the nightmare.

Entering one of the rooms, Ross set her down on the chaise near the windows. "Everything working?" he asked, gently feeling her knee.

Holding back tears—for her mother, not because she was in physical pain—Melanie nodded. "I think I just need to let my heart settle down for a minute."

"What were you doing up on the second floor again?"

"Hoping to find the truth."

"Something in short supply around here," Ross muttered, moving to a cart that held a crystal container and several glasses on a tray.

The room had been made habitable. Noting the blueprints on the drawing table, Melanie realized Ross was using this as his base of operation for the renovation. Though shaky, she was able to get to her feet just as he turned, a glass of amber liquid in hand.

"Have some brandy. And then I want details."

Melanie took the glass from him. A sip and the fire hit her belly. "He tried to kill me again." When Ross rushed toward the door she said, "Don't bother. You won't find him. He's long gone." Then wild thoughts began tumbling out of her. "He's an expert at it, isn't he? This murder thing. I mean, he's created a whole curse. *Him*. He's the curse…murderer of Slater children."

Expression darkening, Ross asked, "How do you know this? Who the hell is it?"

"Instinct. And I don't know who. I couldn't see his face." Another sip of the burning liquid clarified things for her, though. "So I'm the only grandchild to survive the curse. Well, me and Vincent. That is, if he's ever been targeted." Or was he the one doing the targeting? she wondered, knowing he could be. "I think whoever attacked me was the same person who attacked Mom. That scream…"

"Attacked Olivia? How?" Ross took the empty glass from her and set it down.

"Sexually. He had her pinned to a couch." Melanie tried to see him—his face—but it was all so muddled in her mind. Despite the brandy, she felt cold and shaky just thinking about it, almost as if she had been the victim. "Mom struggled, but he was too strong for her...."

Ross put his arms around her and Melanie couldn't hold back. Her emotions were too raw. She clung to him tightly.

"I couldn't see it all the way through, but I know what happened," she whispered. "Is that why Mom broke it off with Webb? Because she was raped?"

Which would make her biological father a rapist. No wonder her mother had never wanted to come back to this house.

"That would explain part of the mystery," Ross admitted, tightening his hold on her.

And it would explain why her mother hadn't wanted Melanie to come here. What it didn't explain was why Mom hadn't put the man who'd violated her in jail.

Seconds ticked by. A minute. More. Melanie didn't want Ross to ever let go of her.

"Make me forget," she said.

He smoothed her back with a long stroke down her spine. "I wish I could."

Remembering how gently he'd kissed her earlier, how much caring she'd felt at that brush of his lips over hers, she said, "You can. I know it."

This time she kissed him. Hard. As if doing so could erase the memory.

Ross's body responded but he tore his mouth

from hers and said, "Melanie, I'm not sure this is a good idea."

She didn't argue, merely kissed him again and slid her body along his so that he couldn't ignore what it was doing to his. Groaning, he seemed convinced and took control, pressing her back into the chaise. A moment's panic threatened to choke her, but she told herself that Ross would never hurt her.

Indeed, as he touched her and stroked her through her clothing, he brought her wave after wave of pleasure. Her breasts yearned for a more direct touch, but when he reached between her thighs—just like in the memory—she stiffened for a moment. But only for a moment. His seductive stroke along the seam of her crop pants made her bring her hips off the chaise and press herself against his hand.

She wanted—no, needed—affirmation that she was still alive. What better way than to make love with a man who'd become so important to her that she was willing to share herself with him?

Even so, between kisses she couldn't help but sneak looks into the shadows, as if *he* were waiting there, ready to pounce the moment they became too caught up in one another to be aware of danger.

Forcing away the terrible memory that wasn't even hers, Melanie chose to replace it with one of her own that she never wanted to forget.

It was only when they were joined in the true sense of the word that everything but Ross slipped from her thoughts. She rolled him, landing on top, then began to ride him hard and fast. He gripped her hips and pushed her upward, half off him.

"Easy."

"I don't want easy. I want it hard and I want it now."

He grinned up at her. "Whatever the lady wants." Then let her have at him as she desired.

They finished in a frenzy. Together. She sank down over him and for the moment felt safe in his arms.

How long would that last? she wondered.

For a while longer, at least.

Ross made love to her again, this time slow and sweet so that she ached for release by the time he gave it to her. Something good to remember.

"I knew you would be like this," he said, cupping her breast and thumbing the nipple through her bra.

She shivered. "Like how?"

"Indescribably delicious."

"Isn't that copy for a candy-bar commercial?" she joked, slipping out from under him to straighten and button and zip the clothes that she hadn't quite lost.

Beautifully half nude in the moonlight, Ross grinned at her as he pulled up his pants. "Too bad we can't shower together down here. The water's off. Then again, there's your room."

"I don't think that's a good idea."

"My being in your room or your relatives seeing us together?"

"Either."

She sensed rather than saw the shift in him.

"They're going to know about us sooner or later," he said evenly, as if he hadn't reacted. "Sooner, actually. Tomorrow night at the party."

Melanie made a face that he probably couldn't see. "Not really."

"What does that mean?"

Her pulse threaded unevenly when she told him, "That I'm going with Andrew."

Another beat of silence. Melanie started to grow uncomfortable.

"You can tell Andrew you changed your mind."

"No, I can't."

Her stomach was suddenly in a twist. She hadn't even told Andrew yet. But—no matter how she felt about Ross—she knew Andrew had to be her escort and for reasons other than to please her demanding grandfather.

Slater House was trying to give her answers, but she had to play her part. She *was* part of it…in her mother's stead. Everything was coming together so vividly in her mind.

Her grandfather was trying to redo her in Mom's image. Instinct told her to go with that. To do all as Mom had done that fateful night. Including attending the party with Andrew Lennox. Surely her grandfather knew more than he'd already told her. Somehow, looking like Mom, Melanie figured she could wheedle it out of him.

"I don't understand then," Ross said, his voice as tight as his posture as he gestured to the chaise. "What was *this* all about?"

"Impulse and the need to feel something other than fear."

"So you would have slept with *any* man who'd showed up so you would feel better?"

Now she was the one who felt insulted. "Of course not!"

"Just one who would have your grandfather's stamp of approval."

Not wanting to have to explain herself, she said, "I need to get out of here."

"Away from me?"

She couldn't say what Ross wanted to hear. She started off without him.

"I'm coming with you," he said, following close behind her.

"I said no."

"Don't worry. I know my place now. But I'm not going to let you wander these halls with a murderer tailing you. So you're just going to have to take your chances that someone sees us together as I escort you to your room."

Melanie wished things could be different between them. But she couldn't tell Ross the plan that was forming in her mind, not without having him interfere.

Ross would never let her go through with her plan to make the rapist/killer nervous enough to come after her again.

THEY WERE TOGETHER. Again.

Hating being thwarted, hating not finishing what

he'd started, he watched from his hiding spot in the dark hallway.

He *would* finish.

This was his destiny. He'd known it starting all those years ago. And he'd had such success, was now so close to his goal.

He wasn't certain what was going on with Melanie, but he sensed she was getting close to the truth. Perhaps she wasn't interested in what she could inherit, after all.

At least Olivia was taken care of. If anyone figured out she hadn't died in that car accident and tried to find her in Chicago, they would simply think she ran away and changed her identity again.

Now the decades-old secret would be safe….

As soon as he figured out a way to take care of the daughter, which he would do the next night under cover of the party.

Chapter Fifteen

"There we go, darling." The blond man in the mirror nearly swooned when he finished working on Melanie late the next afternoon. "Beautiful...beautiful! Don't you love?"

"To tell you the truth, I hardly recognize myself," Melanie said with satisfaction, staring at a reflection that belonged more to her mother than it did to her.

"Which was the whole point of your giving me the photo of your mother, wasn't it?"

"Exactly." Her hair was a silky cascade of red and her makeup was so artfully done that she looked as natural as one of those models on the cover of a fashion magazine. "It's perfect. I can take it from here now."

"May tonight be everything you hope for."

"Oh, it will be, I promise you."

More than that, she promised herself.

The stylist picked up his cases and made for the door, and she pulled the sea blue dress from its hanger.

As far as Melanie could tell, the graduation party

was possibly the last happy day her mother had spent in this house. Which meant it was the night she'd been violated. The man responsible would be here tonight—Melanie was certain of that. She hoped to haunt the bastard into revealing himself. She'd spent the better part of the day getting things in place. If everything went according to plan, when the night was over, she would nail him.

With proof!

The possibilities were limited. Martin. Vincent. Andrew. Johnson. They'd all lived in this house twenty-five years ago. Martin seemed ineffectual, but who knew what he could be like when angered? The very jealous Vincent might be a few years younger than Mom but he'd undoubtedly been much stronger. Andrew seemed to live for Frederick Slater rather than have a life of his own, and Mom had been in love with someone else. Johnson might have imagined a relationship with her mother that went beyond friendship and then when thwarted…

Did the butler do it? she wondered. Could Roger Johnson really be her biological father?

Questions…how many of them would be answered tonight? The identity of the rapist…how that impacted her mother so she'd been forced to run away from the only home she'd ever known…whether or not what had happened to Mom was then somehow connected with the Slater Curse…

Even knowing it was a futile gesture, Melanie tried calling her mother one last time. She didn't bother leaving a message. The idea that Mom had set off to rescue her and yet had never arrived made her sick inside.

If anything had happened to Mom, it would be *her* fault.

She had to fix things. Expose the truth. Nail the man who'd raped her mother and had tried to kill *her.*

Her fault. Her responsibility.

She only hoped when she was done that her mother would appear from wherever she was hiding unharmed.

The house phone rang, freezing Melanie to the spot. Could her mother be calling her at last?

Hand trembling, she picked up, saying, "Melanie here."

"You sound just like her."

Not her mother, but the woman's voice shook a bit. Melanie sat down. "Her?"

"Olivia. When they described you, I knew you looked like your mother."

"Jannie?"

"Oh, I'm sorry. This is Janine Marsh-Evans. I'm in Philadelphia, actually. I've been out of town all week and when I called the store to update the owner, I learned that you'd been looking for me."

Melanie took a deep breath. "I thought maybe you could tell me where to find my mother."

"Olivia? No. I'm sorry, but I haven't seen her since…well, since she left all those years ago."

From her tone, Melanie got the idea that Jannie knew about the rape.

"I thought she was on her way to fetch me home,"

Melanie explained. Undoubtedly that had been Mom's plan. "She never arrived, though. I know she's afraid of someone here at Slater House. I was wondering if you knew who."

Silence.

"This is important," Melanie said urgently. "I know all those years ago, you went out with Roger Johnson. He broke up with you—because of my mother?"

"No, of course not. Why would she want to split up her best friend and her brother?"

"Brother?" Melanie gasped.

"Well, half brother. Frederick and Mildred had a rough patch early on, or so I was told. Roger's mother was their very attractive chief cook."

A fact that no one had mentioned. If Johnson was one of the family, then why had he been relegated to the position of butler? It would certainly explain why he had a sense of entitlement.

"Listen, honey, I've got to go. When you see your mom, you give her a big hug for me and tell her to call me."

"I'll do that," Melanie promised.

She stood staring at the telephone for a moment, realizing Jannie hadn't answered her question about whom Mom might fear. She'd denied it was Roger Johnson, though.

So the butler was her uncle. No one had bothered to inform her, not even him. Having Slater blood and being treated like a servant probably didn't go together too well. Did he hate anyone who carried the Slater name? Enough to kill their children? Their legal heirs? Enough to rape his half sister, no matter what Jannie thought?

Rape wasn't a sexual act. The women she'd interviewed for her documentary were proof of that. Rape was a statement of power.

I'll teach you to defy me!

The words Mom's attacker had used before he'd assaulted her echoed in Melanie's mind.

Well, she was ready to defy the bastard, whoever he was.

Ready or not, Melanie thought, leaving her quarters.

Descending the stairs, she looked for Andrew, who'd said he would wait for her in the conservatory. Indeed, he was sitting next to a rubber tree plant and scanning his Palm Pilot. As if he sensed her presence, he looked up. Standing, he put the Palm Pilot back into the pocket of his white linen suit jacket.

"You look lovely, Melanie. You could be Olivia." He offered her his arm.

Her stomach tightened at the comparison to her mother—she was certain she would get many such compliments from the people who'd known Mom.

"Thank you, Andrew. Shall we?"

Guests were already arriving. Johnson was playing the good butler, guarding the front door, giving his approval to couples and a few singles who entered and crossed the foyer as if they'd done so dozens of times. Which they probably had.

"Do you think we could get a drink before Grandfather introduces me to a roomful of strangers?"

"That can be arranged." Andrew took two stemmed

glasses filled with champagne from a passing waiter's tray. "To an evening well spent," he said.

"I certainly hope so." Melanie drank half the glass, then paused to gauge the effect of the bubbly. "I imagine you'll be working the room."

"Pardon?"

"Your campaign. Helen told me you were planning on running for governor. I expect that takes a lot of personal contact to pull off."

"Indeed."

"You don't seem like the type."

"What type would that be?"

"A politician."

"Family tradition," Andrew said. "Being wealthy doesn't give us the right to sit back on our laurels. We need to give back to this country. We've had Lennoxes in state and federal government for…well, more than a century, I guess. I only hope I have it in me to do what I must."

Such passion she heard in his voice. "It's nice to know that some people still think highly of being a public servant." Especially considering this wasn't a monetary move for Andrew, who was already a wealthy man.

"My only hesitation is that so many administrations are hung with scandal. It makes politicians look bad not only to their constituents but to the rest of the world."

"So you're not planning on creating scandal?"

Andrew laughed and Melanie found herself smiling. She really did like the man.

Nearly as large as the ballroom in the south wing, the room was already filled with guests and more were arriving. Her grandfather's idea of intimate was definitely on a different scale than hers. Long buffet tables were set up with finger food that must have cost a fortune. Round tables that sat a dozen people each covered one end of the room, and she could see more out on the terrace, which had been tented against an impending thunderstorm. At the far end of the room, a quartet played a popular piece.

"Would you care to dance?" Andrew asked.

"Why not?"

That would allow her to move around the room and to see where everyone was without seeming so obvious.

Andrew was a natural on the dance floor and Melanie found she didn't have to concentrate, merely to float in his arms. As he whirled her around smoothly, she tried to spot Ross. If he was already here, he was hidden in the crush.

Part of her wanted to be with him, but the other part knew she had to keep to her plan—to re-create the night of Mom's graduation party as closely as possible. When this was all over, she would explain everything to him.

If only that wasn't too late.

"You'd make any man proud to be seen with you on his arm."

Melanie turned back to her partner...the young Andrew.

"You're such a flatterer, Andrew," I say.

"I'm serious. You do know how fond of you I am, don't you?"

"And I of you."

I mean it, yet I look away from him and around the room until I spot Webb through the crowd. He's wearing a tux, but it's a waiter's uniform. The rift between us couldn't be wider. He's glowering at me, but I know hurt fuels his anger.

I can't stand it any longer. I don't care what Father says, I need to be with him. So I give him the sign, our signal, the one that says he's to meet me as soon as possible....

DRY LIGHTNING startled Melanie back to the present and pulled her gaze toward the terrace.

Ross stood just inside, wearing a pale gray silk and linen suit. Just looking at him, so distinguished, so handsome, sent warmth through her. His gaze was glued to her. He wasn't smiling. The warmth eased and a knot formed in the pit of her stomach. She couldn't take her eyes off him.

She couldn't give him the signal that she wanted to be with him, not yet.

The idea that he might not give her another chance made her chest tighten and her mouth go dry, but she told herself that she could do anything, even convince Ross that she loved him. First she had to re-create that fateful night when she'd been conceived in violence.

She *did* love Ross Bennet—her surety of it surprised even her.

She'd never felt this way about a man before. Maybe because the men she'd dated had still been boys, no matter their ages. Ross was a real man, one who could complete her—he was mature and stimulating, creative and dedicated.

Not to mention downright hot.

What more could a woman ask for?

Instinct pushed Melanie to go to him and damn the consequences, but a sudden realization made her hesitate. Something odd had happened, something significant—she'd had a memory in a room full of people when before it had only happened when she'd been alone. Why?

She hesitated a moment too long.

Ross turned his back on her and slipped out of the room through the terrace doors.

And as another nearby lightning strike outlined his form, Melanie felt her chest tighten. The image of him walking away from her would be burned in her memory like a freeze frame from one of her videos.

"We're being summoned," Andrew murmured in her ear, snapping her back to her purpose. "Frederick is waving us over. I'm sure he wants to show you off."

"Then I guess we'd better let him."

Allowing Andrew to lead her through the crowd, Melanie glanced back at the terrace doors. Ross had disappeared.

He would understand when she explained she'd

simply been following her plan. She had to believe that or she would run after him now and ruin everything.

ROSS SIMPLY COULDN'T take it, so he left the party and headed for his office in the south wing. Maybe he could find something to do that would get his mind off seeing Melanie in Andrew's arms.

This might be a little like how his brother had felt when he'd learned Olivia was pregnant by another man. Webb hadn't known about the rape, so he would have assumed Olivia preferred another man over him.

Gut-wrenching, that's what it was.

Ross couldn't believe Melanie had chosen old money over him, not when she'd been so odd about finding out she had unexpected wealth. Ross knew he was the equal of any man in that room and he believed Melanie had feelings for him, even if she was fighting them. They had so much in common, starting with their obsession with the past.

More importantly, he'd thought she was falling for him the way he was for her.

His mistake?

Lord, he didn't know. He was making a lot of them. Then again, what else was new?

He'd been making mistakes ever since going to Webb and letting him know about Olivia's pregnancy. He'd always suspected Webb had done something about it, something that had gotten him killed.

He couldn't shake that suspicion any more than he could shake the feeling that Melanie was desperate enough for the truth that she would put herself in danger.

He couldn't let anything happen to another person he cared about.

So what the hell could he do to protect her?

ANDREW STOPPED and Melanie turned forward to gaze into her grandfather's smiling face.

"Ah, here you are, my dear. I want you to meet the Witherbees, Alex and Sandra. Alex is CEO of Natural Threads, a local textile business."

"Nice to meet you."

Before she could do more than shake hands, her grandfather was introducing her to the next couple and the next. The Lawrences and the Kramers and the Fitzgeralds. Andrew got left behind. She made a face to tell him she was sorry. He merely shrugged his shoulders and indicated all was fine.

When a woman her mother's age said, "Why, aren't you the spitting image of dear Olivia," Melanie knew her makeover was a success.

"And she's going to stay here, where she belongs," her grandfather said.

"I'm not really sure of that," Melanie countered. "I have a documentary waiting for me in Chicago."

"Melanie has a nice little hobby," her grandfather said, "but as my heir, she'll have other, more important things to see to."

Furious with him, Melanie kept a smile plastered to her face and murmured, "We'll see."

"Well," the woman said, "hopefully you're

smarter than your mother and will listen to your grandfather's counsel."

"Smarter?"

"Yes, look how she ended up. I'm afraid Olivia got exactly what she deserved by aligning herself with someone below her station."

It took all of Melanie's willpower to keep from tossing her champagne into the woman's face.

Thankfully, the bitch moved on and Grandfather got sidetracked for a moment.

Melanie looked around the room, noting each of the Slater House men. Andrew was indeed at work, shaking hands and clapping shoulders like a politician. Martin was the center of attention of a group of men. Every so often, expression closed, he glanced Melanie's way as if keeping track of her whereabouts. Johnson stood at the doorway as if keeping track of everyone—he barely let his gaze sweep over her. Because he didn't want to be obvious?

The only one unaccounted for was her cousin.

When her grandfather turned back to her, Melanie asked, "Is Vincent here somewhere?"

"I did see him earlier. Maybe he went outside for some air." He held out his hand. "May I have the honor of this dance, my dear?"

"Of course."

Still not comfortable with her grandfather's affection, Melanie held herself stiffly away from him. He didn't seem to mind. Smiling indulgently, he moved her to the music, but as she relaxed, he pulled her closer.

"You are so beautiful. Every man in this room must envy me."

"A bit of an exaggeration," she said.

"How could any man resist you?"

He slid a hand along her cheek and to the back of her head, and Melanie suddenly realized his face was coming closer as if he was going to kiss her.

Pulse rushing through her, she pushed at his chest. "Grandfather, what are you thinking?"

"That I would like to take you upstairs and have my way with you."

"What?"

Shocked by the suggestion and by his leering expression, Melanie went cold inside. She shoved her grandfather away and pushed through the crowd.

"My dear, wait for me!"

Melanie couldn't get out of the room fast enough. Her stomach was in a knot and she felt as if she were going to throw up over someone's designer clothing if she didn't get outside quickly enough.

"Melanie, is something wrong?"

She looked up at Andrew, who seemed concerned. "I just need some air," she lied.

What she needed was to never have come here in the first place. To have listened to her mother. To have forgotten all about John Grey and his claims.

Melanie slipped out to the terrace and kept going, but no matter how fast she ran, she couldn't leave behind her grandfather's lewd suggestion.

The wind whipped her skirts around her, nearly

tropical-storm force. Thunder rumbled in the distance, as if the ominous voice of the coming storm laughed at her naiveté.

Dear Lord, why hadn't it occurred to her before? She didn't want to believe it, but this would explain everything…why her mother could never come back here…why her grandfather was so fascinated with her.

The thought was so awful, it was unthinkable, but think about it she did.

Had her grandfather seen Mom as a substitute for his late wife, Mildred?

Had he acted on that?

The air was thick with humidity—imminent rain—making breathing difficult. Or perhaps it was the new knowledge that choked her.

Sick, that was what it would be if it were true. Faced by the possibility, she wanted with all her heart to reject the explanation.

Surely he hadn't forced himself on his own daughter.

Surely Frederick Slater was simply her grandfather, not her father, as well.

Just outside the south wing, Melanie fell to her knees, her stomach heaving with the knowledge that the grandfather she'd come to meet might want either to bed her or to kill her…or both.

Chapter Sixteen

A torrent of rain cut short Melanie's moment of self-indulgence. Weather wrapped the mansion in its wet grip. A crack of thunder followed by a lightning strike served as fair warning: evil lurked in Slater House.

Defiantly, Melanie scrambled to her feet and pitched forward toward a door at the far end of the south wing that for some reason stood open.

Was this where Ross had gone?

Stumbling inside, Melanie realized she wasn't actually in the ballroom, but in a narrow hallway connected to the inner stairwell that she'd noted on Ross's blueprints. One he said the servants had used for discretion.

Looking up into a dark maw at the top of the stairs, she felt her pulse begin to thud.

Familiar…

As if on automatic, she started forward to investigate but her feet didn't want to cooperate. They felt leaden, stuck to the spot, as if they remembered something bad and didn't want to go there again.

Melanie fought the fear.

What was left? she wondered.

What could be scarier than what she'd already faced?

Her body trembled, but Melanie put it to her being soaked to the skin. Whatever was waiting for her, she had to know. She forced herself to move upward.

Concentrating as she took the stairs slowly and deliberately, she felt the shift in time and pushed her mind backward....

"LET GO OF ME!" I cry, horrified that he dare touch me again.

"Or?"

Staring at the buttons on his linen suit jacket so I don't have to look into his evil face, I say, "I'll tell everyone how you attacked me."

"You mean, how we made love?"

I think I'm going to be sick, both from what he says and from his very presence. And from the product of his rape...all-day morning sickness because of the life growing inside me. I can't let him know I'm pregnant or he'll use the innocent child for his own purposes.

Turning my back on him, intending to flee to safety, I gasp, "You raped me!"

"The bastard raped you?"

My heart drops when I hear Webb and look up to see him fly by me as if I'm not here. Before I can stop it, he's attacking. The men collide and whirl around together. Fists pound at flesh. Terrified, I stand here and watch, unable to stop them.

I didn't want Webb to know. Now everyone would.

Suddenly I realize they're at the edge of the stairs. One false step and...

Webb tries to get his balance.

With a sharp, purposeful push from the bastard, Webb goes flying. He tries to catch himself and for a second I see the shock and regret on his face. I scream and run toward him as his body bounces down one stair at a time. Something gives with a loud snap, and when I get to him, his head sits at an unnatural angle and his eyes are open.

His neck is broken.

"We-e-ebb," I scream, throwing myself down to the floor next to him. He's still warm when I touch him, but I know he's gone. Even so, I can't stop touching him, hoping that my hands can heal him, bring him back to life. "You bastard, you killed him!" I say, turning to face Webb's killer.

"It was an accident."

"You pushed him. You're evil and everyone needs to know. You won't get away with this."

"I will if I bury you with him."

Screaming inside my head, I look for an escape. One of the servants left a silver tray on a table in the hall. An unlikely weapon, I grab it and swing it so fast he doesn't have time to lift an arm. The edge clips him in the head and he goes down to his knees groaning.

"I'll get you...last thing...ever do..."

I believe him.

I run.

I want to tell someone, anyone, but will I be be-

lieved? My word against that of a Southern gentle-
man, one with such money and power, such connec-
tions...would he ever pay?

Or would I be trapped in a nightmare from which
I could never escape?

I stumble halfway across the yard and sob out
loud as I look back toward the south wing. No
movement. He must be stunned. I know I have to
grab my car keys and leave...now...and never
come back...

"MELANIE? My dear, are you all right?"

Melanie snapped into the present and looked
down to see a wet Andrew standing a few steps below
her, aiming a flashlight in her direction.

"What are you doing here?"

"Checking on you. I don't believe you are all right.
You look as if you've seen a ghost."

"Maybe I have," she said slowly. "A ghost from
the past."

He nodded. "Yes, it is becoming more difficult to
keep the present straight from the past with you looking so much like Olivia."

Survival instincts telling her to get out of here,
Melanie boldly descended the staircase and tried to
leave, but Andrew blocked the door.

"I'm flattered you want to be alone with me," he
said, reaching out to touch her.

A ripple of fear skitted along her spine and, realizing the truth at last, Melanie ducked the other way,
through the door that led into the ballroom. At least

she had the option of running here. Maybe she could get away from him…but she wasn't about to try before she got some answers.

"What is it you want from me, Andrew?" she asked loudly.

"The same thing you want of me."

"But that's it. I don't want anything from you. I only chose you as my escort tonight to satisfy Grandfather so he wouldn't push someone I didn't even know on me."

"There's more between us than that," Andrew said, trying to take her in his arms. "Surely you've realized it before now."

Nearly engulfed in the same fear she'd felt on the stairs, Melanie shoved him away and stepped back. "It was you, wasn't it?" she asked. Not her grandfather, who probably was suffering some kind of dementia that allowed him to confuse her with Mom and his late wife. "You raped my mother and killed Webb Bennet. *You* are the Slater Curse."

Lightning seemed to curtain the wing, making Andrew glow a silver gray. His features contorted into something unrecognizable when he said, "Pity that you figured it out."

To Melanie's horror, Andrew Lennox had just admitted that he was her biological father, not that it seemed to register with him.

"This cover-up business is so tedious," he went on. "You should have stayed in Chicago. Now I'll have to get rid of you, as well."

"As well as who—my mother?"

Andrew merely laughed. "Olivia is such a weak woman."

"Where is she?"

"You're assuming she's still alive."

He was enjoying this—torturing her. Melanie made tight fists. She wanted to smash one into him, but she remembered how strong he was.

"What is it you want? Money? I have plenty of it. I can get you millions."

Not that she even knew if she could get her hands on a single dollar without her grandfather's approval. But if Andrew was greedy enough to believe it…

"I have all the money I need. I want what I've always wanted, what I've planned for all these years. Slater House, of course. It's the perfect house for a future president. American royalty. And this is truly a palace on American soil."

Melanie realized Andrew was delusional. "And you think you'll get it how?"

"By eliminating the rest of my competition. After I rid myself of you, there will only be Vincent and Martin to worry about. Then all the Slaters will be gone."

"You've killed her, then?" Melanie's voice broke and tears quickly filled her eyes. "My mother is dead?"

"I may not be a Slater," Andrew went on, allowing Melanie's uncertainty to linger. "But my sister is. I am the head of Frederick's legal team, remember. I'll be executor of the estate of a man whose mind is lost to Alzheimer's. After that, it won't take much to be the owner in truth. You didn't know your grandfather was losing his mind, did you? He was diagnosed recently. The reason he sent John Grey to find Olivia and then you…he wanted to get to know you before it was too late."

Grey had said Grandfather was sick and wanted to have his family around him before it was too late. Melanie had merely assumed he'd had a bad heart or some other physical ailment, and she'd been furious when she thought she'd been manipulated into believing something that wasn't true.

Crushed by the weight of her mistaken conclusions about her grandfather's actions, already mourning the loss of her mother, Melanie was off her game when Andrew grabbed her by her long hair and twisted it around his hand. She saw stars and as he moved her back into the inner hallway between the ballroom and outside walls, she was barely able to put up a fight.

"What are you going to do to me?" she asked, hoping that making him talk would give her some wiggle room.

"Make sure you disappear for good…just like your mother."

Melanie struggled—elbowed him and kicked out, connecting with his shin, but he had a good grip on her head and smashed it into the side of the wall. Stunned from the blow, she could hardly stay on her feet.

Andrew opened a door and shoved Melanie inside. Unable to find any footing, she reached for anything to break her fall.

"I'll be back to take care of you later," he threatened.

Her hand met a railing and she gripped it hard and jerked to a stop. "You won't get away with this!"

Andrew merely laughed and slammed the door shut, leaving her alone.

All the mistakes she'd made, all the wrong conclusions, were locked in the dark with her. If she ever had the chance to know her grandfather, she swore she would make it up to the poor man. And Roger Johnson. The butler hadn't done it, after all. Knowing Andrew's plans for Vincent and Martin, she even felt a brush of pity for them.

She couldn't even think about her mom. Not now, not until she could mourn her properly.

They all had to be warned. All the remaining Slaters. She had to get out of here. Taking a few deep breaths, she tested herself to see if she were steady on the steps.

Suddenly she felt another presence nearby. The short hairs on the back of her neck stood at attention as she recognized the vibe.

"Mom? Omigod, are you really alive?"

ROSS HADN'T BEEN ABLE to settle down in his office, after all, so he found himself back at the party. While he spotted a damp-looking Andrew—the lawyer must have been out on the terrace when the sky opened—there was no sign of Melanie. Figuring she must have made a trip to the powder room, he settled in to wait for her to make a reappearance. One way or the other, he was going to talk to her, maybe even tell her how he felt about her.

If that actually would mean anything.

"Alone tonight?" Helen asked, coming up behind him.

"Afraid so."

"I thought for certain you and Melanie would be together."

"The chemistry's that obvious?"

"Maybe not to everyone. But Melanie herself gave me a head's up when she asked me about you. That girl is smitten…." Helen's gaze was troubled. "The reason I couldn't understand her being with Andrew tonight. Did the two of you fight?"

"Only after she told me Andrew would be her escort for the evening. Could be she's just going for the gold."

"That doesn't sound like Melanie."

No, it didn't. So what was the point of her going with old Lennox money? Something to do with the past? If so, why wouldn't she have told him?

"Odd that Andrew would be interested in someone as young as Melanie," he said. "I remember him escorting her mother to some of these functions."

Helen frowned and murmured, "Yes, he thought Olivia was the perfect woman for him."

"Personally, or for his career?"

Unnerved at his direct question, she said, "I'm not comfortable with this conversation, Ross. Perhaps you ought to take up your concerns with my brother."

Even though there was something in her tone that put Ross on edge, he nodded politely and took his leave of the woman.

After scouring the room and the terrace and still not seeing any sign of Melanie, Ross started to worry for real. A trip to the powder room didn't take this long.

Slipping out of the banquet hall, he quickly made his way upstairs. The servant underground had informed him she was staying in the Rose Suite.

But she wasn't there, either.

Moving to her terrace doors, he stared out at the south wing, barely visible through another onslaught of rain until lightning struck a little too close for comfort. The abandoned wing had enough structural problems without getting zapped. Surely Melanie hadn't gone there to pry more secrets from the past.

He returned to the party, hoping to find her.

No Melanie.

But he spotted Roger Johnson across the room, directing a couple of waiters carrying trays of champagne and appetizers to different areas of the room.

Ross approached the butler and caught him between duties. "Do you have a minute?"

"Certainly, sir."

"Knock off the formality, Roger. You didn't call me sir the time you gave me that bloody nose."

"One you well deserved, if I remember correctly."

"A matter of opinion."

"Of course. What can I do for you?"

"Tell me where Melanie's gone off to."

"I was wondering the same myself."

Interesting that the butler had been keeping track. "So you haven't seen her?"

"Not since she rushed off the dance floor. I believe Mr. Frederick was having one of his off moments and took her for Miss Mildred."

"Off moments." Ross had recognized something

going on with Frederick. Little disturbing things that never lasted long enough to add up. Only they were starting to now. "Do these moments happen often?"

"Unhappily, more often with each passing week."

"Sorry to hear that."

Ross really was. He might have issues with the old man, but he would rather fight someone in his right mind. Plus that would be devastating for Melanie to find her grandfather only to watch him lose his grip on reality.

"Well, I wonder if Melanie's date for the evening knows where she's off to." Not that he wanted to ask Andrew about it.

"Mr. Andrew went after Miss Melanie, but he came back alone."

"Came back from what direction?"

"I believe it was from the south wing."

Where else?

Thunder rumbled so close, Ross took it as a warning. He glanced out the windows as the sky lit. The south wing glowed unnaturally.

"Thanks, Roger."

A last look around the room assured Ross that Melanie was not here.

And now, neither was Andrew.

MOM WAS ALIVE!

Melanie had found a switch that provided them with enough light to see each other. Her mother wasn't moving fast thanks to Andrew, who must have smacked her head against something hard and had thrown her down the stairs, leaving her to die. His M.O., she guessed. Nothing seemed to be broken, but Mom was limping, and Melanie didn't like the lump on her head, either.

"We need to get out of here and get you checked out by a doctor, Mom."

Here being the old wine cellar still filled with casks.

"I'm all right. Just bruised."

Of course the door was locked. Above, the timbers seemed to shake every time thunder rumbled. Maybe it had something to do with the low ceiling and their proximity to the earth. They were below ground.

Being trapped in here gave Melanie the willies. No memories, just a dreadful feeling she couldn't shake. Like maybe if she didn't find a way out, this would be their grave.

The far reaches of the cellar remained dark, making her wonder if there were other light switches to be accessed. She started to explore, hoping to find a way out.

Having told her mother about the memory transference, she asked, "How did Andrew get you alone that night?"

"I was a bit drunk. I wasn't legal, but Father didn't stop me from having some champagne. I got Webb to meet me upstairs. We were innocent, really, but we still had to steal moments to be together. Webb left first—we always were discreet that way—then when I started to leave, Andrew stopped me. He'd been watching us."

"Some kind of pervert," Melanie muttered, finding another light switch.

Another section of cellar lit, revealing dozens upon dozens more wine casks, but it didn't seem there were any doors or windows offering a way out this damn place. A trickling sound brought her face-to-face with a leak. A narrow ribbon of water was flowing down one of the walls and puddling on the floor. As far as she could tell, there was nowhere for it to go.

If the storm kept up, would they have to worry about drowning, too?

"We argued about my betraying him," her mother went on, "and he demanded that I commit to him. *Marry* him. He already had Father's approval. I told him I loved Webb and…"

Circling back to her mother for moral support, Melanie said, "I pretty much know the rest of what happened." She didn't need the exact details, the reason she'd pulled herself from the memory when she'd experienced it. "Why didn't you do anything then?"

"I was afraid. Father worshipped Andrew, wished he was his son. He kept pushing me at him, insisting he was a man worthy of a Slater daughter. I feared that if he knew I'd lost my virginity to Andrew—who, by the way, claimed it was consensual—Father would force me to marry him."

That comment about their *making* love. "Bastard!" Melanie swore vehemently. She could hardly believe the villain was her biological father.

"Andrew can be very convincing. I almost think he believes it himself. Father certainly would have given his story credence, because he would have wanted to believe it. After what happened, I couldn't be with Webb, so I broke it off with him. And then I didn't know what to do."

"So Andrew never learned you were pregnant with me?"

"No. That's all he would have needed to trap me. And then, when Webb overheard us, and Andrew pushed him down those stairs…" Her mother shuddered. "Andrew's family connections, political connections, would have closed ranks around him, and Webb's death would have been declared accidental. I'm sure of it. Andrew would have gotten away with murder, and I *still* might have been his prize. Father thought more of Andrew Lennox than he did of his own daughter."

"That's not true. Grandfather loves you, no matter how difficult he was. Is. You have to believe that, Mom. When he spoke of you, thinking you were dead, he had tears in his eyes."

Melanie put her arms around her mother and they held each other tight for a moment. She could imagine how terrified Mom had been as a vulnerable young woman. Melanie had experienced some of that firsthand.

Mom patted her back and pushed her away so they could look each other in the eyes. "Honey, *you* were the one thing good that came of a horrible experience. I've never regretted *you*. As far as I'm concerned, I have the best daughter in the whole world and I would be lost without you."

Now there were tears in Melanie's eyes. She hugged her mother again.

"I have the best Mom, so that makes us even."

Mom *had* been the best parent in the world, one who'd loved and protected her child, even before she was born. Always. Now it was Melanie's turn to protect her mother. She had to find a way out of this mess, had to find a way to get the justice Mom hadn't been able to get for herself.

"There has to be another way out of here," she reasoned. "A service door of some kind. Those casks didn't get down here through that door." Melanie indicated the one at the top of the stairs.

With every minute that passed, the feeling of urgency increased. It was as if the house were warning her.

Get out…get out…get out now while you still can.

Melanie swept around the outer walls up close and personal this time. The rain drumming against metal sounded like a heartbeat. Where was that coming from? Following the sound, she got to the far back reaches of the cellar before realizing part of the wall appeared to be makeshift—almost like one of the screens she'd found upstairs. She moved the panel out of the way of a wide service door.

"Mom, look. Maybe we can get this open."

"Too bad you won't have time to try."

Melanie whipped around and looked to the stairs and the man standing there. Her eyes widened at the gun in Andrew's hand. If only they'd had a little while longer…

Their time was up. What now?

How was she going to keep her own father from killing them?

ANDREW WAVED THE GUN from Melanie to Olivia. "I'm assuming you would prefer dying together."

"I don't plan to die at all," Melanie said, cocky. She strolled slowly back toward Olivia.

"I don't care what you're planning—"

"Even if it gets you what you want?"

"And that would be?"

"This house."

Andrew laughed. "How do you propose to give me the house? A wedding gift perhaps?"

"What? You're suggesting I should marry my own father?"

"Mel, no," Olivia cried.

Andrew frowned as he took in what Melanie was intimating and Olivia's apparent distress. "Larry Pierce was your father."

The girl stopped next to her mother and squeezed Olivia's shoulder. "There was no Larry Pierce."

"But Grey's records—"

"Lied."

"No, my Larry died just before Mel was born—"

"Give it up, Mom. Andrew knows the truth now."

Of course he did. "Then Webb Bennet—"

"No," Melanie interrupted. "You…seduced… Mom, and I was the result. So whatever I get from Grandfather is yours. You can have my share of the house on one condition. You let me and my mother live."

Andrew didn't know whether or not he should believe it…Melanie his daughter?

Possible, he guessed, even though he and Olivia had only been together that one time. Was that why she had run away, to keep his daughter from him?

Melanie…he'd felt a connection to her all along. Looking at her, she was Olivia all over again. But inside, she was more. She was hard and determined. She was him. And what she was offering was very, very tempting…if he could believe she would go through with it.

He asked, "How do I know you'll make good on your word?"

"You're a lawyer," Melanie said, moving closer. "I'm sure there are some kind of legal papers you can draw up, right? You can do it now. Keep us locked here until you draw them up. I'll sign them, I swear. Then you can let us go."

Andrew didn't think quickly enough. Melanie got too close. She rushed him and tried to get the gun. Reflex made him squeeze the trigger and a shot rang out, the blast echoing through the cellar.

"Aah!"

Melanie flipped around and screamed "Mom!" as Olivia crumpled to the ground.

"At last your mother can have what she always wanted," Andrew said. "Eternity with her lover."

Chapter Seventeen

Ross had just taken refuge from the storm when a clap of thunder shook the house.

No lightning illuminated the inside of the ball-room.

Then what the hell was that?

Stomach knotted, he moved to the outside wall, to where a hidden door led to the servants' staircase.

He opened it and heard Melanie scream, "Mom!"

Mom? *Olivia?* Olivia was alive?

"You shouldn't have tried to fool me, bitch."

Andrew's voice. Ross moved silently to the wine cellar entrance, whose door stood open.

"She's still alive," Melanie said, voice breaking on a sob. "We have to get her to a doctor."

Andrew said, "She's not going anywhere. And neither are you."

Ross's cue. Halfway down the steps, he flew over the remaining ones at the other man's back and landed on him so hard that they both crashed to the cellar floor. Gun still in hand, Andrew rolled and aimed wildly.

Another shot went off and took a chunk out of a rotting support in the middle of the casks. The house protested as Ross got hold of Andrew's gun hand and dug his fingers into the flesh with great force until the bastard let go.

The gun went skittering across the floor and Melanie lunged for it.

His free hand sliding around Ross's neck, Andrew squeezed so hard he cut off Ross's air and conjured up stars. Then the bastard rolled over him. Suspecting Andrew was about to bash in his head—the way he had John Grey's?—Ross grabbed the other man's most vulnerable parts and twisted. With a strangled cry, Andrew let go and pulled off him.

Gasping in air, Ross struggled to his feet. He only wished Olivia had known that trick when Andrew had made his intentions clear all those years ago.

"Ross, are you all right?" Melanie asked.

"I will be. Olivia?"

"Her pulse is weak, but she's alive.'

"Really big surprise."

Before he could demand an explanation, Andrew was on his feet. He threw himself at Ross and they flew back in between rows of empty wine casks, rotting timbers and supports everywhere, a particularly vulnerable area due to years of water damage and neglect.

Andrew might be a dozen years his senior, but he was a fit man and as strong as hell. Having experienced the strength of those hands once, Ross kept away from them as much as possible.

He danced around the other man, moving in only to throw a few punches. Andrew punched back, connecting with Ross's jaw, and when Ross was momentarily stunned, Andrew turned him and jabbed him in the kidneys.

More stars. Gasping, Ross went down to one knee and though he saw Andrew aim a foot to kick him, couldn't move.

"Stop right there, Andrew, or I'll shoot!"

Ross glanced up at Melanie standing with both hands aiming the gun at Andrew.

Andrew froze. "You think you have the nerve to kill me, Melanie? You don't even know how to use a gun properly."

"Didn't I tell you about the documentary I did on handguns? Part of the deal was that I went to a firing range and got quite expert with several models."

Ross caught his breath, pushed the pain to the back of his consciousness and stumbled to his feet.

Andrew's expression was one of fury. "You should have died at the waterfall."

"You should have been punished for what you did to my mother and Webb," Melanie returned. "Ross, he's the one who killed your brother. I saw him do it."

"You couldn't have seen it," Andrew snarled. "You weren't even born yet."

The offhand admission made Ross see red. He flew at the murdering bastard, knocked him back into a support that gave with a crack. The house moaned in protest. Andrew's fist came out and clipped Ross, sending him flying backward. Then the support toppled, knocking Andrew into the wine casks.

Ross scrabbled back as one beam fell with a screech, then another, setting a disaster in motion. The stacked casks seemed to sigh with resignation before rolling down like a set of round dominoes, trapping Andrew, and—unless the bastard was due a miracle, which Ross didn't believe he was—crushing him to death.

Melanie still stood frozen with her hands around the gun. Ross couldn't read her expression.

"The house," she murmured, "the only thing he ever cared about stopped him dead. In a way, he got his wish. Now he belongs to Slater House forever."

"CAN I GO IN the ambulance with my mother?" Melanie asked anxiously as the EMTs prepared to move her some time later.

"Sorry, ma'am, you'll have to take your own car."

"But what if…" She couldn't put her greatest fear into words. Instead she asked, "What if she needs me?"

"Mel, honey, I'll be fine," Mom protested. "I'm not going to die on the way to the hospital."

Melanie only wished she could be so sure after what had gone on here this night. Thank God Ross had had his cell phone and it had worked despite the storm. He'd also called up to the house and had informed Johnson of what had gone down.

The investigative team had already arrived. Ross had given one of the detectives the short version and

Melanie had promised full cooperation as soon as her mother was taken care of. Now a couple of the crime scene investigators were checking out the accident site.

"I'm from Chicago," she told one of the paramedics. "I don't know where to find the hospital."

"I'll take you," Ross said, his tone unnaturally cool.

"Thanks." She squeezed her mother's hand as a burly man and a small woman half his size lifted the stretcher. "Mom, I'll see you at the hospital."

"I'll be waiting for you, Mel."

The team slowly negotiated the stairs. Melanie glanced over at the area where Andrew lay flattened under the rubble. Men were carefully clearing the debris, trying to get to the wine casks, so they could pull them off his body.

She couldn't get Andrew's comment about her mother having eternity with her lover out of mind. What had he meant by that? He'd meant to kill them and then what? Drag them out of here to bury them?

Or...

She gasped.

"What?" Ross asked.

"Your brother... I think he's down here."

"You think Andrew buried him in the wine cellar?"

"No, not buried."

Melanie approached the wine casks and thumped one in the side. Then the next and the next. They all sounded the same...empty.

Just then the casks in the pile on Andrew shifted and twisted unnaturally. Nothing had happened to make them move like that.

Only the house...

Melanie stepped forward and looked down at what was left of the man responsible for her existence.

She wanted to feel something. Anything. But looking at Andrew Lennox left her cold inside. She'd never met a worse human being, not even in her worst documentary-making moments.

But he had nothing to do with making her who she was. She had her mother to thank for that.

"Hey, miss, watch it there," one of the investigators warned her. "It's not safe."

"I'm safe here," she murmured.

Feeling as if she were one with the building that had shared so much with her, Melanie imagined the south wing had been protecting her, protecting all of them, while seeing that justice was finally done. She reached out, hand hovering, then went for the cask directly on Andrew's chest.

A simple tug and the end popped out.

And with it, a skeletal arm.

THEY WERE ALL GATHERED at the hospital. Well, some of them. Grandfather. Roger Johnson. Martin.

But Melanie felt alone—Ross had dropped her off and left, saying he needed to talk to the detectives. She'd been checked over by a doctor. Bruised but not badly hurt. Not like her mother had been.

"Our little girl is going to be all right, Mildred," her grandfather suddenly whispered in her ear. "Don't you worry your pretty head."

"No," she said faintly, realizing how often her

grandfather was straying from reality. "No reason to worry now."

A nurse entered the waiting room. "Mrs. Pierce can have visitors."

Melanie went in first. To her relief, Mom's color looked good, and though she was hooked up to an intravenous drip, she was sitting up in bed, sipping water through a straw. And when she saw her daughter, her face lit in a smile. Melanie hugged her gently, then sat on the edge of the hospital bed.

"Hey, Mom, the doctor says you're going to be all right, that it was just a flesh wound."

"Tell my aching side that." Mom's smile faded. "Mel, what were you thinking coming here?"

"That you were afraid for good reason. If Grey found you, anyone else could have. I had to figure out why and try to fix things."

"You always were a stubborn little girl."

"I take after my mother. The others are outside. They want to see you."

"If I must."

"You don't have to do anything you don't want to do, Mom. But Grandfather is really upset. He's confusing me with your mother."

"What?"

"He's losing it, Mom. Alzheimer's. I don't know how you feel about seeing him, but if you want any contact with him while he still remembers you, now is probably a good time to start."

Her mother's eyes suddenly grew watery. "All right. I'll see him."

"And the others? Martin? Johnson?"

She nodded. "Send my brothers in, as well."

Melanie did as her mother asked.

What now? she wondered.

Her questions were answered, her mother was safe. Did she just go back to Chicago as if none of this had ever happened? Like she didn't have a grandfather and other relatives, some of whom had been kind to her?

Like Helen, who had turned out to be her aunt for real, not just by marriage. And who had sadly just lost the person most dear to her. Helen had lost so much because of him. Or Johnson, who should be seen as more than a butler at Slater House. With someone on his side, he had so much to gain.

Not that it was her responsibility to fix things. Been there, done that.

And yet...

Her musings were interrupted by Ross's arrival with the lead detective. Melanie's heart went into overdrive as he took her aside.

"How is Olivia?"

"Mom'll be fine, thankfully."

"Why didn't you tell me she was alive?"

"I—I couldn't, Ross. I hated it, but it was her secret to reveal, not mine."

But Melanie could see that explanation didn't wash for him. She wanted to tell him the rest—why she hadn't gone to the party with him—but before she could broach the subject, he backed off.

"I'll leave you to give your statement," he said, turning to leave.

"Ross, wait."

"Later."

With a sense of helplessness greater than she'd ever felt, Melanie watched the man she loved walk away from her. She swallowed her fear that this could be the last time she saw Ross. He had said *later.*

Making good on her word, she told the detective everything that had happened starting with Grey finding her on the shoot and ending with, "If you need proof, send one of your men up to the balcony over the ballroom. You'll find my camcorder between the rails up there. I got the truth out of Andrew. The camcorder should have started recording at the sound of our voices."

The detective thanked her and left.

At which point, Melanie realized her grandfather was waiting for her with Johnson. She wondered how much of her story he'd overheard. If anything she'd said had upset him, she couldn't tell.

All he said was, "Let's get you home, Melanie."

"I don't want to leave Mom."

"Miss Olivia doesn't want you to stay here all night," Johnson said. "She was very firm that we should take care of you."

"Thanks…Uncle Roger."

The butler looked taken aback for a moment, then a pleased smile made his lips twitch.

As they left the hospital, she looked around for Ross, but there was no Jaguar.

What was she going to do about him?

That was the uppermost question on her mind.

She'd been certain she could explain her intentions for the night and that he would listen, but he hadn't even given her the chance. And maybe he never would.

No sign of the authorities when they got to Slater House. Inside, all was quiet. The guests had gone and, despite the crisis, the servants had efficiently cleaned up.

Her grandfather stopped in front of the elevator that would take him up to his third-floor suite. "Tomorrow is the first day of the rest of your life," he said. "I promise it will be better than today."

"Anything would be."

"We'll go to see Olivia together and have a serious discussion, the three of us. It's time she moved back here where she belongs."

"That's for her to decide."

"But she'll want to be with you."

"Grandfather, I have a life in Chicago. I have my work there."

"Work that you can do anywhere, especially when you have the funds to make that happen. You can have all the money you want, do whatever you want—"

"Money isn't everything," she interjected. "I know that must come as a shock to hear. I've done okay on my own, you know. All I ever lacked was family."

"Which you now have."

"A dysfunctional one."

Her grandfather laughed. "All families are dysfunctional. Please, Melanie. I don't know how much time I have left to get to know you. Give me that honor."

He sounded so humble, she almost gave in. Then

she remembered how well he manipulated people, including her.

"You'll try to control me and I'm not someone who'll put up with it."

"Then we'll have an interesting time, won't we? Please. I want my daughter and her only child in my life."

Though she felt badly about his disease, she wasn't ready to make any promises. "I'll think about it."

"Good," he said, smiling as he turned to step into the elevator car.

Undoubtedly he thought he'd won. And maybe he had.

Now that the secrets of the past had been revealed and she could be her real self, she wanted to try again. Her only hesitation was Ross. Obviously he'd given up on her without a real fight.

She wandered through the dining room to the terrace, stopping when she realized she wasn't alone. Ross was standing there, as if waiting for her.

"Are you going to leave me, too?"

Her pulse rushed at his presence. "It depends on what you want of me."

"Everything."

She knew he wasn't talking about money. Her chest tightened. "I don't know if I'm ready for everything."

"Then I'll take what you'll give me until you do know. And you will know in time, Melanie, because we're meant for each other."

"You're not still angry about tonight? I mean, about my not going to the party with you?"

"I got it, Melanie. It wasn't the smartest thing you've ever done, but I understand where it came from."

"It didn't have anything to do with you," she promised. "Or with the way I feel about you."

"How do you feel about me?"

She grinned at him. "Why, the same way you feel about me."

Melanie slipped into Ross's arms and looked out at the south wing. The rain had long stopped and the moon was out. The wing glowed brightly, looking just like part of any old big mansion. It was if the rain had washed the evil from Slater House.

In a way it had, Melanie thought, wondering how her mother would feel about having quarters in that wing—ones designed especially for them to wipe out the bad memories. If anyone could do it, that would be the man she loved and who so obviously loved her.

"Tomorrow is the first day of the rest of our lives," Melanie said, echoing her grandfather. "Anything can happen."

"I'll make sure that it does," Ross said, nudging open her lips with his.

Her spirits lifting for the first time since she entered Slater Woods less than a week ago—surely a man with such creative drive and determination would figure out a way to make good things happen—Melanie kissed him in return.

The house sighed.

**Hidden in the secrets of antiquity,
lies the unimagined truth...**

Introducing

a brand-new line filled with mystery
and suspense, action and adventure,
and a fascinating look into history.
And it all begins with DESTINY.

In a sealed crypt in
France, where the
terrifying legend of
the beast of Gevaudan
begins to unravel,
Annja Creed discovers
a stunning artifact
that will seal her destiny.

*Available every other
month starting
July 2006, wherever
you buy books.*

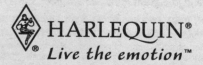

If you enjoyed what you just read,
then we've got an offer you can't resist!

Take 2 bestselling
love stories FREE!

Plus get a FREE surprise gift!

Clip this page and mail it to Harlequin Reader Service®

IN U.S.A.
3010 Walden Ave.
P.O. Box 1867
Buffalo, N.Y. 14240-1867

IN CANADA
P.O. Box 609
Fort Erie, Ontario
L2A 5X3

YES! Please send me 2 free Harlequin Intrigue® novels and my free surprise gift. After receiving them, if I don't wish to receive anymore, I can return the shipping statement marked cancel. If I don't cancel, I will receive 4 brand-new novels each month, before they're available in stores! In the U.S.A., bill me at the bargain price of $4.24 plus 25¢ shipping and handling per book and applicable sales tax, if any*. In Canada, bill me at the bargain price of $4.99 plus 25¢ shipping and handling per book and applicable taxes**. That's the complete price and a savings of at least 10% off the cover prices—what a great deal! I understand that accepting the 2 free books and gift places me under no obligation ever to buy any books. I can always return a shipment and cancel at any time. Even if I never buy another book from Harlequin, the 2 free books and gift are mine to keep forever.

181 HDN DZ7N
381 HDN DZ7P

Name	(PLEASE PRINT)	
Address	Apt.#	
City	State/Prov.	Zip/Postal Code

Not valid to current Harlequin Intrigue® subscribers.

Want to try two free books from another series?
Call 1-800-873-8635 or visit www.morefreebooks.com.

* Terms and prices subject to change without notice. Sales tax applicable in N.Y.
** Canadian residents will be charged applicable provincial taxes and GST.
   All orders subject to approval. Offer limited to one per household.
   ® are registered trademarks owned and used by the trademark owner and or its licensee.

INT04R   ©2004 Harlequin Enterprises Limited

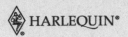

INTRIGUE®

COMING NEXT MONTH

#927 COVERT MAKEOVER by Mallory Kane
Miami Confidential

Weddings Your Way consultant Sophie Brooks is good at her job. Love is another story. So when she crosses paths with Sean Majors while trailing a kidnapper, it's not just Sophie's life that's in grave danger. But her heart, too.

#928 RAPID FIRE by Jessica Andersen
Bear Claw Creek Crime Lab

Criminologist Thorne Coleridge suffers flashes that help him solve crimes. But are they enough to save his former protégée Maya Cooper from a roaming serial killer that may have connections to one of Colorado's finest?

#929 DUPLICATE DAUGHTER by Alice Sharpe
Dead Ringer

When Katie Fields travels to Alaska to connect with the mother she never knew, the woman is nowhere to be found. And the only man that can help isn't talking. If he had a choice, he'd be content just raising his daughter. Good thing for Katie, he doesn't.

#930 SECRETS OF HIS OWN by Amanda Stevens
Cape Diablo

Holed up in a Spanish villa nestled off the Gulf Coast, Nick Draco holds a secret that no one can ever know. But when a search for a dear friend leads Carrie Bishop to his doorstep, the truth will be revealed, and no one's life will ever be the same.

#931 EVIDENCE OF MARRIAGE by Ann Voss Peterson
Wedding Mission

After being kidnapped, Diana Gale realized she couldn't rely on anyone but herself for protection. Not her ex-fiancé, Reed McCaskey. And not her father, imprisoned murderer Dryden Kane. But with a copycat killer on the loose, it might be best for her to reconsider before it's too late.

#932 THE CRADLE FILES by Delores Fossen

Lexie Rayburn held a gun on Garrett O'Malley but didn't know why. Was he really the father of her baby girl? Could he help her find the people that took her baby? And did she really have amnesia?

HICNM0606